JANA COULDN'T BELIEVE SHE AND RANDY WERE THROUGH.

This was it. The moment she had been dreading. She slowed down and then stopped as Randy caught up with her, but she didn't turn around or look at him. "I know you have something to tell me. Go ahead. Get it over with."

"What are you talking about?" he asked. "I don't have anything to tell you, and I don't understand why you're acting like this."

Jana spun around. "Oh, no? Well, I know better. I know that you're just waiting for the chance to break up with me. So why don't you just leave me alone and go back to your *new* girlfriend, Laura McCall!" she cried.

Before Randy could answer, she whirled away again. Running as fast as she could to get away from him, she headed across the street.

Suddenly the air was filled with the sound of screeching tires. Or was it someone shouting her name? She felt a hard jolt, and the pavement rushed to meet her. Then everything went black.

Bantam Skylark Books by Betsy Haynes
Ask your bookseller for the books you have missed

THE AGAINST TAFFY SINCLAIR CLUB
TAFFY SINCLAIR STRIKES AGAIN
TAFFY SINCLAIR, QUEEN OF THE SOAPS
TAFFY SINCLAIR AND THE ROMANCE MACHINE
  DISASTER
BLACKMAILED BY TAFFY SINCLAIR
TAFFY SINCLAIR, BABY ASHLEY, AND ME
TAFFY SINCLAIR AND THE SECRET ADMIRER
  EPIDEMIC
TAFFY SINCLAIR AND THE MELANIE MAKE-OVER
THE TRUTH ABOUT TAFFY SINCLAIR
THE GREAT MOM SWAP
THE GREAT BOYFRIEND TRAP

Books in The Fabulous Five Series

1 SEVENTH-GRADE RUMORS
2 THE TROUBLE WITH FLIRTING
3 THE POPULARITY TRAP
4 HER HONOR, KATIE SHANNON
5 THE BRAGGING WAR
6 THE PARENT GAME
7 THE KISSING DISASTER
8 THE RUNAWAY CRISIS
9 THE BOYFRIEND DILEMMA
#10 PLAYING THE PART
#11 HIT AND RUN

THE FABULOUS FIVE

Hit and Run

BETSY HAYNES

A BANTAM SKYLARK BOOK®
NEW YORK · TORONTO · LONDON · SYDNEY · AUCKLAND

RL 5, 009-012

HIT AND RUN
A Bantam Skylark Book / August 1989

*Skylark Books is a registered trademark of Bantam Books,
a division of Bantam Doubleday Dell Publishing Group, Inc.
Registered in U.S. Patent and Trademark Office and elsewhere.*

ISBN 0-553-15746-9

Published simultaneously in the United States and Canada

*Bantam Books are published by Bantam Books, a division of Bantam Double-
day Dell Publishing Group, Inc. Its trademark, consisting of the words
"Bantam Books" and the portrayal of a rooster, is Registered in U.S. Patent
and Trademark Office and in other countries. Marca Registrada. Bantam
Books, 666 Fifth Avenue, New York, New York 10103.*

PRINTED IN THE UNITED STATES OF AMERICA

O   0 9 8 7 6 5 4 3 2 1

Hit and Run

CHAPTER

1

"What do you like best about Randy Kirwan?" Melanie Edwards asked Jana Morgan as the two friends sauntered out of the Wakeman Junior High cafeteria. "Romantically speaking, that is," she added, and winked.

"For goodness' sake, Mel," said Jana, rolling her eyes. "Can't you ever think of anything but boys?" It always amazed Jana that Melanie had crushes on three or four boys at a time and was constantly on the lookout for someone new.

Melanie grinned. "Sure. But why should I? Seriously though, I'm trying to decide what the perfect boyfriend should be like, and since you and Randy have been going together since sixth grade, naturally I decided to check with you."

Jana couldn't help chuckling to herself. She couldn't imagine Melanie's ever settling for just one boyfriend, perfect or not, but Jana thought over Melanie's question anyway. She liked everything about Randy. How could she possibly come up with one thing she liked best? "Well, he's totally sincere," she offered. "And he's nice to everybody whether they're popular or not."

"Is he a good kisser?"

Jana knew Melanie was teasing, but she blushed anyway. "Of course, but there are lots of other special things about him, too."

"Come on. Keep thinking. I need a longer list than this," said Melanie.

"Hi, you two. What's up?" asked Beth Barry as she, Katie Shannon, and Christie Winchell came up behind them.

"Melanie is giving me the third degree about why I like Randy," answered Jana.

"You're kidding," cried Beth. "What for?"

Raising one eyebrow, Katie turned to Melanie. "Are you planning to steal him?"

"Of course not," Melanie huffed. "What I'm doing is making a checklist so that I can evaluate cute boys and find out what kind of boyfriends they would make. That way I'll know when I've found the perfect guy. I need a couple of dozen items to check off, but so far I've only gotten three from Jana. Randy's sincere. He's nice to people, and he's a *terrific* kisser."

"What!" shrieked Jana. "That's not what I said."

Melanie widened her eyes, faking a look of innocence. "Do you mean he's *not* a terrific kisser?"

Jana gave Melanie an exasperated look and turned to Beth. "What about Keith?"

"He's understanding," Beth said softly, and Jana knew she was referring to the problems they had had when Beth was in the school play.

"Yeah," said Jana. "So is Randy, and he's also loyal. You know. He doesn't flirt with other girls."

"Which he could do very easily if he was that type of guy," added Melanie. "I mean, he is *sooo* gorgeous that any girl would go bananas if he paid attention to her."

"Watch it," Jana cautioned playfully. "Do you know what I'd do to any girl—including YOU—if I found out she was making a play for Randy?" Grinning, Jana ran her index finger across her throat and made a slashing sound. "Murder and mayhem!"

Melanie held up her hands in surrender. "I'm innocent. I'm just making a checklist. Remember?"

"Well, you'll have to make your checklist without me for the rest of lunch period," said Jana. The girls had stopped at the door to the school ground and were about to go outside as they did most days after lunch. "I just remembered that I left a book in the yearbook room yesterday after school, and I need it in my next class. See you guys later."

Jana left her friends and headed down the hall toward the yearbook room thinking about Randy. There was no other boy she had ever met who could begin to compare to him, and Melanie would be lucky if she found someone half so special. Jana smiled to herself as she remembered how she had had his sixth-grade school picture blown up to poster size and had kept it thumbtacked to her wall. Each night as she fell asleep, she could gaze at his handsome face, dark, wavy hair, and sparkling eyes by the glow of her night-light.

There had been other things that had made their romance special, too. For instance, they had gotten each other's name in the computer matchup back in Mark Twain Elementary, and they both loved deep-dish, pepperoni, green pepper, and mushroom pizza. She sighed. They had so much in common it was as if their love was meant to be.

The yearbook room was deserted when Jana stepped inside, and yet the chaos of trying to assemble a pictorial history of the school year was visible everywhere. Schedules were taped to the walls. Boxes of pictures and stacks of notes and lists covered the tables used by the various editorial departments.

Jana headed for the long table she shared with her seventh-grade coeditor, Funny Hawthorne. Somewhere under the piles of class pictures was the Family Living book she was looking for.

Just as she passed the sports desk, an action shot of last week's football game caught her eye. Stopping, she picked it up and felt a glow of pride at the sight of Randy dropping back to complete a pass.

As she stood looking at Randy's picture, she was aware of little snatches of conversation coming from students walking in the hallway, but one voice drifted into the room and forced its way into her consciousness.

"Randy is such a doll. I'll just die if he doesn't tell her about us pretty soon so that . . ."

Jana shot to attention, her eyes riveted to the open doorway and the hallway beyond. Who had said that? The voice—a girl's voice—had passed just out of earshot before she had finished speaking. What had she meant?

Dropping the picture, Jana raced to the door and looked out. Her heart pounded as she scanned the hallway in the direction she had just come. Except for two ninth-grade boys scuffing along, there was no one there. This is silly, she told herself as she looked in the other direction. It's a free country. Anyone can talk about Randy if they want to.

At that instant she saw two girls turning a corner at the far end of the hall. One was short with dark hair, but the other one was tall. Her long blond braid started at the top of her head and fell over her shoulder. Jana froze. *Laura McCall*. She had been the one talking about Randy, and the girl with her was Tammy Lucero, one of Laura's best friends and also the biggest gossip in Wakeman Junior High.

Jana sank against the doorframe. Maybe she had misunderstood. Maybe it was another Randy that Laura had been talking about. But what was it that Laura wanted him to tell *her*? And could the *her* possibly be Jana? She shook her head. Laura couldn't have been talking about Randy Kirwan, that's just all there was to it. And she couldn't possibly have meant that she was waiting for Randy to tell Jana that he liked Laura now instead of her. Or that he wanted to break up with her. Could she?

CHAPTER

2

*W*hen the bell rang, Jana headed for her Family Living class in a fog of hurt and anger. Was something really going on between Randy and Laura, and had she simply been too blind to see it? Her heart ached, and she sank into her seat in the classroom going over and over in her mind every single thing that had happened between herself and Randy during the past few days. They had talked in the halls and at Bumpers. They had gone to the movies together on Friday night. He seemed the same as ever, she thought. He hadn't acted as if he were trying to tell me something. Or worse. That he doesn't like me anymore.

By the time school was dismissed for the day and she was heading for her locker, Jana had been over every instance when she had even so much as glimpsed Randy in the halls between classes for the past week, trying to remember if she had seen him talking to Laura. She had replayed all their conversations in her mind for any memories of his mentioning Laura's name. She was just about to answer no to all of them when she remembered entering homeroom one morning last week and seeing Laura and Randy standing together. They were talking quietly, but was that all? The memory was hazy. It seemed as if he was handing Laura something. A pencil? A piece of paper? *A note?*

Jana swallowed hard and leaned against her locker, closing her eyes to shut out distractions while she tried to conjure up a clear picture of that moment. She couldn't. No matter how hard she strained to see into the memory, the images wouldn't sharpen enough for her to tell what had really happened.

Someone caught Jana by the arm. "Are you okay?" It was Katie.

Jana turned to look at her friend. "Yes," she said. "I mean no. I don't know what I mean." She shrugged and let out a deep sigh. By this time the rest of The Fabulous Five had gathered around her, and each of them gave her an encouraging smile. Melanie, Christie, Katie, and Beth had been her best friends practically forever, and they had always been there when she needed them. They had helped her back in Mark Twain Elementary School each time her enemy Taffy Sinclair had tried to take Randy away from her. Now Jana needed The Fabulous Five more than ever.

She shook her head as she tried to fight back tears. "I think I'm losing Randy," she blurted out.

"Oh, come on. That's impossible," said Beth. "Whatever gave you a silly idea like that?"

The others were nodding, agreeing with Beth.

"You guys didn't have a fight, did you?" asked Melanie.

Jana tried to speak around the catch in her throat, but the words jerked and bumped as they came out. "No . . . nothing like that . . . but at lunchtime . . . when I went to find my book . . . I overheard . . ." She stopped, fighting back another wave of tears. Wiping her eyes with the back of her hand, she went on, spilling out the words in a single breath. "I overheard Laura telling Tammy Lucero that she would die if Randy didn't tell me about the two of them pretty soon."

"You're kidding," cried Christie.

"She's lying," Beth said firmly. She stepped forward and put an arm around Jana.

"That's right," said Katie. "She just wanted you to hear it and get jealous."

"She didn't know I heard it," insisted Jana. "That's what makes it so awful. I was in the year-book room, and she and Tammy were walking by in the hall. There was no way she could have known I was there. And now that I think about it, I can remember seeing Randy and Laura together in home-room one morning last week, and he was giving her something. A note, I think. I don't know why I didn't realize something was going on between them."

No one said anything for a moment, and then Christie spoke softly. "Now that you mention it, I saw them in the media center yesterday. They were by the card catalog, but I don't think they were looking up anything."

"Who knows?" said Melanie. "Maybe they've been assigned to work together for a class."

"Right," said Katie. Her voice rose excitedly. "That could even be why Randy gave her the note."

"Sure," Jana said without enthusiasm. "That would explain everything except for what Laura told Tammy. If it was something innocent like a school project, why would she act as if it was such a big secret? And why would she be so anxious for him to tell me?"

No one had an answer for that.

"Come on," said Beth. "Let's go to Bumpers. We can talk about it some more on the way."

By the time they left the school building, almost everyone else had gone. Only the sound of an occasional locker banging shut echoed in the halls. As Jana fell into step with her four best friends for the short walk to Bumpers, she thought about Funny Hawthorne. Her friendship with Funny was growing stronger every day, even though Funny was one of Laura McCall's best friends and a member of Laura's clique, The Fantastic Foursome. Jana had a hard time thinking of Funny as a part of the group that was constantly fighting with The Fabulous Five. Somehow she didn't seem to belong.

Does Funny know anything about Laura and Randy? Jana wondered. And if she does, will she risk her friendship with Laura to tell me?

Jana was still thinking about Funny when they reached Bumpers. Kids were streaming into the popular junior high hangout, and she was immediately separated from her friends by a group of eighth-grade boys bulldozing their way toward the order counter.

"Rats," she muttered as she sidestepped around a yellow bumper car with football players hanging over the sides and headed in the direction she thought her friends had gone. She hoped they had found a table somewhere in this madhouse.

Squeezing between the old Wurlitzer jukebox and a group of girls made up of Lisa Snow, Sara Sawyer, and Kim Baxter, plus some others she didn't know, Jana found herself staring straight at Randy. She stopped cold. A chill went through her body, but at the same time heat blazed up her face. He wasn't looking at her. He was looking at the person sitting next to him in the booth. And he was laughing. The person was Laura McCall, and she was laughing, too.

Jana whirled around and plowed through the crowd before he could notice her and see the hurt look on her face. She ducked around booths and bumper cars until she spotted Katie's red hair through a maze of faces on the other side of the room.

"There she is," she heard Beth call as she got near their table. "Over here, Jana," Beth yelled, and waved to her.

Jana sank into the chair they had saved for her and buried her face in her hands. She wanted to cry. It was true. Randy really did like Laura instead of her. Otherwise, why would he be with her now?

"Jana, are you okay?" asked Melanie.

"What happened?" demanded Beth.

Jana balled her hands into tight fists and answered through clenched teeth. "It's Randy. He's sitting with Laura McCall."

"Oh, no!" burst out Christie. "That rat. Who does he think he is?"

"Uh-oh," warned Katie. "You can ask him yourself. Here he comes."

Jana could see Randy making his way through the crowd and heading straight for their table. Her heart was pounding. "Well, he's not going to sit with me," she said angrily. "I'm going home. I'll call you guys later."

Sweeping her books into her arms, Jana jumped to her feet and hurried toward the door. She could hear Randy calling her. "Wait!" he cried. "Hey, Jana. Wait up!"

She didn't stop. The last thing she wanted right now was to talk to him. She pulled open the door and ran into the afternoon sunlight.

Randy was right behind her. "Jana, will you slow down and tell me what's wrong?"

This was it. The moment she had been dreading. She slowed down and then stopped as he caught up with her, but she didn't turn around or look at him. "I know you have something to tell me. Go ahead. Get it over with."

"What are you talking about? I don't have anything to tell you, and I don't understand why you're acting like this."

Jana spun around. "Oh, no? Well, I know better. I know that you're just waiting for the chance to break up with me. So why don't you just leave me alone and go back to your *new* girlfriend, Laura McCall!" she cried.

Before Randy could answer, she whirled away again. Running as fast as she could to get away from him, she headed across the street. Tears blinded her. She didn't want him to follow. She only wanted to get away. To get home where she could think and sort everything out.

Suddenly the air was filled with the sound of screeching tires. Or was it someone shouting her name? She felt a hard jolt, and the pavement rushed to meet her. Then everything went black.

CHAPTER

3

*E*ven before Jana opened her eyes, she was aware of the pain in her head. It was a fierce, stabbing pain that throbbed in time with her heartbeat. She wished that she could pull the dark, warm blanket of sleep back up over herself and return to the comfortable oblivion she had just come from, but her head hurt too badly. And there were sounds. Voices.

Slowly she forced her eyelids open, but it didn't help. Everything was fuzzy.

"Mrs. Pinkerton, come quickly," someone called. "She's awake."

"Oh, Jana, honey. How do you feel?"

Jana looked toward the second voice, and her eyes gradually focused on her mother's face. A woman in white stood just behind her.

Mom? she tried to whisper. She felt her lips part, but no sound came out.

"Don't try to talk, honey," her mother said. "Just lie still. Everything is going to be all right."

Where am I? What's happening? Jana wondered. She tried to turn her head and look around, but it hurt too much.

As if she had read her daughter's thoughts, Mrs. Pinkerton stroked Jana's hair and said, "You're in the hospital, sweetie. There was an accident. A car. But don't worry. The doctor says you're going to be fine. You have a concussion from hitting your head on the pavement and some bumps and bruises. That's all."

Jana could hear her mother crying softly. She wanted to ask her to explain more. What accident? What car? And if she was going to be okay, why was her mother crying? But her head was still pounding, and she was sleepy. *So* sleepy.

When she awoke again, the room was dark except for a sliver of light coming in through the half-open door. "Mom!" she cried, and tried to sit up in an instant of panic.

"Yes, Jana. I'm right here, and so is Pink."

Her mother's and stepfather's faces materialized

out of the shadows and seemed to float over the side
of her bed like a pair of gently bobbing balloons.

"Just lie back, honey," Pink said softly. "Everything's okay."

Gratefully, Jana sank back onto her pillows. "Oh,
wow. I'm dizzy," she said, trying to smile.

"And you're probably hungry, too," said Pink.
"I'll ask the nurse to get you a tray."

He hurried out of the room as her mother
switched on the bedside lamp. The soft light illumi-
nated the hospital room, and Jana got the first
glimpse of her surroundings. There were two beds,
the one she was lying in, which was by the window,
and an empty one nearer the door. A sink and a mirror were on the wall opposite the beds, and a door
that she assumed led into the bathroom was beside
the sink. She wrinkled her nose. The whole place
had a strange smell. Maybe it was medicine. Or dis-
infectant. Or both. A shiver went through her. This
looked just like the hospital room her grandmother
had been in a couple of years ago, she thought, remembering how cold and unfriendly her grandmother's room had seemed to her then.

Mrs. Pinkerton took Jana's hand. "Do you remember what happened?" she asked gently.

Jana started to shake her head, but the pain
rushed back again. "No," she said instead. "At least
I don't think so."

"You were crossing the street in front of Bumpers this afternoon after school," her mother began. "You and Randy. And a car came speeding around the corner and . . ." Sobs broke off the sentence.

Suddenly a picture flashed in Jana's mind, and she sat up abruptly in spite of the pain. She and Randy had been in front of Bumpers. She remembered now. They had been arguing. She frowned. About what? She and Randy never argued. Well, almost never. Then more of the scene came back. They had been arguing about Laura McCall, and Jana had run into the street in anger. But she had been alone.

"Randy!" she cried, searching her mother's face. "Randy wasn't . . . I mean, I don't think . . . I mean, I don't know. *What happened?*"

Mrs. Pinkerton wiped her eyes. "No one is sure. The police think that Randy pushed you out of the way of the car, and that's why you fell and struck your head on the pavement."

Jana frowned and touched her forehead only to find a huge lump the size of an egg. It hurt to touch it, so she closed her eyes, trying to see into her memory and remember the accident, but she couldn't. "What about Randy? He's okay, isn't he?" she demanded.

Her mother looked away for an instant and then said gently, "Randy is still unconscious. The car hit him, knocking him into the air, and then kept on going. It was a hit-and-run. That's why we don't know exactly what happened."

"But he's going to be all right, isn't he?" Jana insisted, nodding furiously in spite of the pain in her head. Her chest was heaving, and her heart felt as if it were going to burst. "Well, *isn't* he?"

"Yes, dear. I'm sure he will be." Mrs. Pinkerton turned away, and when she looked back, her eyes were bright, and there was a spot of high color on each cheek. "That isn't exactly true," she began slowly. "I have to tell you the truth. Sweetheart, Randy is in critical condition. He has some broken ribs and some internal injuries, but worst of all he hasn't regained consciousness since the accident. The doctors hope he'll wake up, but they can't be certain he will."

Jana felt as if her whole body was caving inward as her mother's words echoed in her mind. *Critical condition. Hope he'll wake up. Can't be sure. Critical condition.* Jana heard a moan and knew it must be her own voice. Closing her eyes, she let the tears flow.

Looking back on it later, she could only vaguely remember what happened next. Her mother holding her in her arms and rocking her, whispering that everything was going to be okay just as she had done so many times when Jana was small. Pink wiping her hot, tear-streaked face and trying to get her to "eat a little something so that at least your tummy will feel better." The nurse coming in to check her and giving her a glass of water. And finally, her mother brushing a lock of hair off her forehead and saying, "The nurse says we have to go now, sweetheart, so that you can sleep. But I'll see you in the morning. Oh, yes, I brought you something so that if you wake up in the night, you won't feel alone."

Jana watched dreamily as her mother reached somewhere behind herself and brought out Gorgeous, the white, cuddly bear Randy had given her for Valentine's Day. He had a red, heart-shaped mouth and black, heart-shaped eyes, and he held his arms out as if he were waiting for a hug. As badly as she hated to be left alone, she smiled gratefully at her mother as Mrs. Pinkerton tucked Gorgeous under the covers beside her.

Turning toward him, Jana hugged him tightly. "Oh, Gorgeous. I'm so glad you're here," she whispered as she drifted off to sleep. "Beautiful, beautiful Gorgeous . . ."

CHAPTER

4

"Rise and shine." The cheerful words were punctuated by the flashing on of the overhead light and the sight of a smiling nurse looking down at her.

Jana squinted into the brightness. She had been in a deep sleep, and when she tried to move, her body hurt all over. Then she remembered where she was and why she was there. The argument with Randy. Running into the street. The screech of tires followed by nothing but blackness until she woke up in the hospital.

"Randy!" she cried. She tried to sit up but was stopped by a new pain that ran from her left shoul-

der all the way down her body. "Is he . . ." But before she could finish her sentence, the nurse was
advancing on her with a thermometer in her outstretched hand.

"That's a good girl. Open up so that I can get your
temperature," she said cheerfully, sliding the thermometer under Jana's tongue. "There'll be plenty of
time for conversation after that."

Jana clamped her lips around the thermometer
and glared at the nurse whose name tag said MRS.
FOSS. How dare that woman refuse to let her talk?
She had to find out about Randy. She pushed the
thermometer to one side of her mouth. "I need to
know about Randy Kirwan!" she insisted, almost
spitting the thermometer into her lap.

The nurse frowned at Jana, but then her expression softened. "Oh, my," she said. "Is Randy the
young man who was in the accident with you?"

Jana pulled the thermometer out of her mouth and
nodded in spite of the pain in her head. "How is he?
Did he wake up? Please. You've got to tell me."

"I wish I could, dear, but he's not my patient. I
believe he's still in the intensive care unit on the second floor. You'll have to speak to someone there.
Sorry," she added, patting Jana's hand. "Now let's
try to get your temperature again."

Obediently, Jana opened her mouth and let Mrs.
Foss slide the thermometer under her tongue again

as a million questions swirled in her mind. Was Randy awake? Was he in pain? Was he going to be okay? And what about the driver of the car? Had they found him yet? Was he in jail? How could he have done a thing like that? It was all his fault that Randy was hurt so badly. He must be some kind of maniac, she thought angrily.

Mrs. Foss busied herself plumping Jana's pillows and straightening her covers. Suddenly she pulled Gorgeous out from somewhere near the foot of the bed. Jana gasped around the thermometer. She had forgotten all about him.

"I see you invited a friend to sleep over," the nurse said with a smile, placing him in Jana's outstretched arms and then removing the thermometer from her mouth.

Jana hugged the soft, white bear gratefully. "Thanks," she said. Then she added, "You said that Randy is on the second floor, didn't you?"

"That's right, dear," said Mrs. Foss as she read the thermometer. "In the intensive care unit."

Jana frowned as she watched the nurse enter Jana's temperature on her chart. How was she going to talk to anyone in the intensive care unit about Randy? She couldn't call and ask—she didn't have a phone in her room.

"Someone will be in with your breakfast tray in just a few minutes," said the nurse. "You stay right where you are for the time being. The doctor will be in later this morning, and he will decide when you can get out of bed."

Jana waited until the nurse left the room. Then, ignoring the warning that she should stay in bed, she moved Gorgeous aside, and slowly pulled herself into a sitting position. It took all her effort to swing her legs over the side of the bed. Every inch of the left side of her body screamed at her with pain. The palms of her hands were badly scraped, and her entire elbow was terribly tender. At least the pain in her head was fainter this morning, but even it was still there. She instinctively raised her hand to feel the knot on her forehead, which was as large as before.

"I've got to find out about Randy," she said to Gorgeous as she tucked him into her place in bed.

Gorgeous looked back at her with his bright black eyes and smiled at her with his heart-shaped mouth, making her forget her pain for a moment. It was the same smile that had won her heart the instant Randy had handed him to her and whispered, "Happy Valentine's Day."

"He's *gorgeous*!" she had cried as she swept him into her arms.

"Really? That's a funny name for a bear," Randy had teased, and they had both burst out laughing.

From that moment on, his name was Gorgeous,

and he had always been there whenever she needed him. She had cried into his soft, plush fur at times when she was sad. She had danced around her bedroom with him in her arms when she was happy. And she had even complained bitterly to him whenever Laura McCall had made her life miserable. She could never ask for a better friend. Now she swallowed hard and looked at him through brimming tears. "I'll be back as soon as I can," she promised.

She hobbled to the metal closet and took out her bathrobe, slipping it on. Then she paused just long enough to look at herself in the mirror over the sink. A soft gasp left her lips as she saw her face for the first time since the accident the day before. The knot on the left side of her forehead stood out like a small antler ready to sprout, and the same side of her face was scraped and bruised purple.

She had turned and was limping slowly toward the door when the icy floor made her realize that her feet were bare. Her bedroom slippers were in the closet, and she stepped into them and headed for the door again. A wave of dizziness swept over her, and she caught the wall for support. "Wow," she whispered. "This is going to be tougher than I thought."

Jana looked back at Gorgeous. He was watching her with arms outstretched and a smile of encouragement. "Okay, Gorgeous," she called to him. "I'm going, and I'll be okay. I'll find out everything I can about Randy and come right back. Don't worry." As she turned away, she almost thought he waved.

Her optimism was short-lived. When she stepped into the hallway, it was far from deserted with nurses bustling in and out of rooms and the breakfast cart clanking slowly along. She pressed herself against the wall, trying to become invisible. What if someone stops me and wants to know where I'm going? she thought. It's a chance I'll just have to take. It's the only way I can find out about Randy.

Her next problem was locating the elevators that would take her to the second floor. She had been unconscious when they brought her in, so she had no idea in which direction to look. To her right was the nurses' station. Two nurses stood there with their backs to her, talking together. There was no sign of any elevators in that direction. Jana looked to the left. An exit sign, lit up in red, hung at the end of the hall. That must be where the elevators are, she thought, and slowly inched her way toward them, wondering if she should go up or down.

It hadn't occurred to her to ask which floor she was on or even to look out her window to see how high up her room was. Fortunately, she reached the elevators without a challenge from anyone and

found the number four painted on the wall beside
them.

Jana punched the down button and glanced back
over her shoulder. Still, no one was paying any attention to her. So far, so good, she thought, crossing
her fingers behind her back for luck.

When the elevator doors opened and a white-
coated doctor stepped out, Jana panicked again. But
he didn't seem to notice her, and she ducked inside
and rode down to the second floor alone.

The second-floor hallway was quieter than her
own, but still her heart was pounding when she followed the arrows and reached the intensive care unit
around the corner from the elevators. Jana paused,
suddenly light-headed, and leaned against the wall
until the feeling passed. The red-haired nurse sitting
at the desk in the nurses' station was intent on her
paperwork and had not looked up.

Jana's heart was in her throat as she glanced toward the glass-topped door beside the station. The
words NO ADMITTANCE WITHOUT AUTHORIZA-
TION were painted on it, and through the dark glass
she could faintly see electronic monitors and
screens, which she knew were there to keep track of
the patients' breathing, heart rate, and other vital
signs. They looked like the ones she had seen on
television programs.

Randy's in there, she thought, as she tiptoed toward the door. Her knees felt rubbery, and the door seemed as if it were getting farther away instead of closer.

What's happening to me? she wondered. The dizzy feeling was getting stronger. If I could see him, she thought. Just for a minute. Just long enough to be sure he's okay.

"Young lady. Stop at once. You can't go in there."

The nurse's words slammed into Jana, stopping her cold.

"I . . ." she began. "I need to see Randy Kirwan. I have to find out if he's okay."

"I'm sorry, but he is not allowed visitors," the nurse said a little more gently.

"But did he wake up yet?" Jana insisted. "Is he going to be all right?"

"I'm sorry," the nurse said firmly. "I'm not allowed to give out any information at this time."

"But I have to know!" Jana cried as anger swelled inside her. "Why won't anyone tell me what's going on?"

The red-haired nurse got slowly to her feet. Glaring at Jana, she said, "Young lady, this is a restricted area. If you do not leave at once, I will call security and have you . . ."

Jana stared at her for a moment, trying to understand the words. But she couldn't. They were fading away and being replaced by a crackling sound in her ears like static on a radio. At the same time, the entire scene was swimming before her eyes. She reached out for something to grab on to just as her knees buckled and she fainted dead away.

CHAPTER

5

*J*ana drifted in and out of consciousness. She felt strong hands lift her off the floor and place her on a gurney. Next she heard the rattle of the gurney's wheels as it moved along the hallway, then the hum of the elevator. Finally, she was in her bed again, and Gorgeous was there beside her.

Opening her eyes, she saw another face looking down at hers. She blinked to focus and realized that the face belonged to a doctor and that he was bending toward her, concern showing clearly on his face.

"Now she's awake," he said as if it were a big event that he had been waiting for. "Hello, Jana. I'm Dr.

Vermillion." He turned on a tiny flashlight no big-
ger than a ballpoint pen and held it near her face,
shining the light into first one eye and then the
other. Every once in a while he would say, "Um
hum," to himself and nod. Finally he switched off
the light and straightened up. "No harm done," he
said, "but I must insist that you remain in bed for
the time being."

Jana could see Mrs. Foss standing behind the doctor and was relieved that she didn't shake her finger
and say, "I told you so." Instead she smiled sympathetically, then turned to the doctor and said, "I'll
see to it that she eats a little breakfast and then
rests."

For the next hour people paraded in and out of
Jana's hospital room, leaving her little time to think
about Randy. Mrs. Foss brought in her breakfast
tray and stood tapping her foot impatiently while
Jana drank her orange juice and milk. After the
nurse left, she totally ignored the poached egg and
only nibbled at the toast. This is worse than the food
in the Wakeman cafeteria, she thought, wrinkling
her nose.

An orderly cleared her tray a little while later, and
then Mrs. Foss stepped back into the room and announced in a singsong voice, "Bath time!" Pulling
the curtain around Jana's bed, she proceeded to help
her get cleaned up for the day.

"You're going to be getting a roommate in a few minutes," said Mrs. Foss.

Jana blinked. "A roommate?"

"Sure," replied the nurse. "A little girl. She was in an automobile accident, too. They'll be bringing her up in just a few minutes."

After the nurse left, Jana looked at the empty bed beside hers. She hadn't thought about having a roommate, even though it did make sense. She wondered if Randy had a roommate in the intensive care unit or if he was in there all by himself. That would be awfully lonely, she thought. Especially at night after his parents went home. She frowned, not wanting to imagine him all alone in that dark room, hooked up to all those monitors she had seen through the window, but she couldn't help it.

She lay there thinking about Randy again for what seemed like ages. If only she had been able to see him in the intensive care unit. She tried for the millionth time to remember the accident, but she couldn't. All she knew was that Randy had tried to save her without thinking about himself, and now he was badly hurt.

Just then the door opened and her mother came in.

"Hi, sweetie. Pink had to go on to work, but I thought I'd stop by for a little while," she said, bending down and kissing Jana on the cheek. "How are you feeling this morning? The nurse said you got up when you weren't supposed to and fainted. Is that true?"

Jana nodded. "I'm okay, though, but what about Randy? Nobody will tell me anything!"

Her mother shook her head. "First tell me what happened. Why did you get out of bed?"

Tears welled up in Jana's eyes. "I wanted to see Randy for myself. I went to the intensive care unit, but they wouldn't let me in. Please tell me. Is he awake yet?"

Mrs. Pinkerton's expression was troubled. "I haven't seen his parents yet. I'm sure they're with Randy. The hospital still isn't giving out much information. All they would tell me when I stopped at the desk downstairs was that his condition hasn't changed."

"That means he isn't awake yet, doesn't it?" she whispered. She wanted to add, *and that he might die*, but she couldn't make herself say the words out loud.

"Don't worry, sweetheart. The doctors are wonderful here, and they're doing everything they possibly can."

Jana nodded. She knew her mother was trying to make her feel better, but nothing could do that except news that Randy was finally awake and getting well.

"Well, I'm certainly glad that you're okay. I have some news," her mother added brightly. "First, I ordered a telephone for your room so that I can call and check on you from work. How does that sound?"

"Terrific," Jana said. And I can call the intensive care unit and check on Randy, she thought.

"Also," her mother went on, "the phone rang off the wall last night. Everybody wanted to know how you were, including all of The Fabulous Five. They not only called to ask how you were, but they're all coming to see you today after school. They sent messages, too. I wrote them down, but it will take a minute to dig them out of my purse."

Jana sighed. It did make her feel better to know that her friends were all concerned about her, and she was glad that they had sent messages. But just as Mrs. Pinkerton began looking through her purse, there was a sharp knock on the hospital room door.

It's probably my roommate, thought Jana as her mother set her purse down beside her chair and called, "Who is it?"

"The police, ma'am," came a husky voice. "I'd like to talk to Miss Morgan about the accident, if I may, please. It will only take a few minutes. I just need to get some information."

"The police?" Jana cried, looking questioningly at her mother.

"It's all right, honey," replied Mrs. Pinkerton as

she opened the door and ushered the policeman into the room.

"I'm sorry to disturb you," said the officer. He was a big man with graying hair, and his kind smile made Jana relax a little. "However, we're investigating the accident, and we need anything you can tell us about the car that struck Randy Kirwan. The driver still hasn't come forward, so we're hoping that witnesses can give us the clues we need to find him. I'd appreciate anything you can tell me."

Jana lowered her eyes. "I didn't see the car," she admitted. "I didn't see anything. I just heard the tires squeal and felt a shove . . . I guess that was Randy pushing me out of the way." Her voice rose to a tiny squeak as she choked back tears. She had never felt so helpless in her life. "The next thing I knew, I was here."

"It's okay, miss. Don't cry. You just lie there and get well. We're doing everything we can to locate the driver. And you can bet we'll find him, too. In fact, I'm going to interview all of the kids who were at Bumpers when the accident happened. Maybe one of them saw something."

"Oh, my gosh, look at the time," said Mrs. Pinkerton as soon as the officer had gone. "I didn't realize it was getting so late. I'd better get to work." She paused, looking lovingly at Jana. "I really hate to leave you."

"That's okay, Mom," Jana assured her. "I'm not on my deathbed or anything, and you do have a job."

"Thanks for understanding, sweetheart. I didn't even get time to find the messages from your friends. I promise to find them and call you during my lunch break. How's that?"

"Super," said Jana. Then with a smile she added, "I'll be right here in this bed. I promise."

Jana stared at the door after her mother had gone. She couldn't stop thinking about Randy. She had known him for practically her whole life, and even before she had liked him as a boyfriend, she had liked him as a friend. He was kind and sincere and he would never hurt anybody on purpose. That was what made the accident so terrible. How could anyone hurt him?

She smiled to herself, remembering that when she was in Mark Twain Elementary she had kept a small notebook hidden in the toe of an old bedroom slipper in the back of her closet. In that notebook she had written down every single thing she ever found out about Randy. Things such as: His full name is Randal Spencer Kirwan. His birthday is January 31. His father is an electrician, and his name is Robert. His mother sells real estate, and her name is Helen. He has an older sister, Kathy, who is in college, and a registered keeshond dog named Heidi. The license plate number on his father's car is RK 4097.

There were a lot of other things she knew about him, too. Things she had found out after they started dating. Mainly, they were things the two of them had in common such as favorites. Deep-dish, pepperoni, green pepper, and mushroom pizza. Amusement parks and riding the roller coaster. Going to the beach and watching fireworks on the Fourth of July. But now maybe they would never get to do any of those things together again. Never eat pizza together or ride a roller coaster or watch fireworks.

Wiping a tear from her eye, Jana suddenly felt very sad. She longed to be home in her own familiar bed instead of here in the hospital where nearly everyone who came into her room was a stranger. But more than that, she wanted things to be back the way they were before. She wanted to roll back the clock to yesterday afternoon before the accident. Maybe even to lunch period when she was alone in the yearbook room.

If I could just be back there, I wouldn't even listen to people talking in the hall, she promised herself. And if I heard Laura talking about Randy, I would just ignore it. And I'd ignore it when I saw them together at Bumpers. And I would never, *never*, never run out into the street. If I could go back and do all that, then right now Randy wouldn't be lying in a hospital bed two floors below hurt so badly that he hasn't awakened since the accident. "It's all my fault," she murmured over and over again.

Her head was beginning to throb again, and the dizzy feeling she had just before she fainted was back. Burying her face in Gorgeous's round body, she was crying softly when she heard the door to her room open and a child's voice shriek, "I won't stay in here! You can't make me! I want my mommy and daddy!"

CHAPTER

6

*T*he first thing Jana saw when she looked up was a gurney being wheeled in by the same orderly who had taken out her breakfast tray an hour or so earlier. In the middle of the gurney lay a tiny little girl about five or six years old with an enormous cast on her leg. Her eyes were red from crying and she was propped up on one elbow, making a terrible face at Mrs. Foss, who was leading the gurney into the room.

"I *said* I want my mommy and daddy!" the little girl screamed, shaking her long blond curls violently.

"I know you did, sweetheart," said the nurse in a soothing voice. "Your mommy and daddy can't see you right now. They're in a room just like this one in another part of the hospital, and just as soon as the doctor says it's okay for them to have visitors, you'll get to go see them. I promise. I'll take you myself."

Mrs. Foss tried to ease the child off the gurney and onto the bed while she talked, but the little girl pounded the nurse with both fists and made loud, snuffling sounds. Finally, after succeeding in getting her into bed and tucked under her covers, Mrs. Foss turned to Jana and said, "This is Lisa Pratt, Jana. She's going to be your roommate for a while. She's had a terrible experience, and she's very frightened right now. Maybe you can talk to her and make her feel a little more comfortable."

Poor little girl, Jana thought, but before she could say anything, Lisa looked straight at her and stuck out her tongue. "I want my mommy and daddy!" she demanded. Then her eyes grew large. "Bear! Bear!" she cried excitedly. "Give him to me."

Instinctively Jana drew Gorgeous closer to her. "I'm sorry, Lisa," she said gently. "You can't have him. He's my bear, and he's very special. Maybe the nurse can find you another bear in the toy box in the playroom."

Lisa began to wail and point to Gorgeous. "Bear! Bear!" she shouted between sobs. "I want *that* bear."

Mrs. Foss bent close to Jana and whispered, "Could you let her borrow it for a few minutes? Her parents were hurt badly, and the family is from another state. They were traveling across country when another car crossed the center line and hit them head-on a few miles outside of town. So you see, there isn't even anyone to visit Lisa until some of her relatives can make the trip here. Your bear might make her feel better."

Jana looked at the nurse in horror. "But . . . I couldn't . . ." she sputtered. She didn't know how to explain that she absolutely could not let some strange little girl borrow Gorgeous. Not the bear that Randy had given her, and not while he was lying in the intensive care unit in critical condition. She needed Gorgeous more than Lisa ever could.

She tried to look away from Lisa, but she couldn't. The little girl's red-rimmed eyes held her fast, pleading with her. Lisa had stopped crying now, but her chin quivered and every few seconds a hiccup shook her frail body. "Please," she said in a tiny voice. "Can't I just hold him?"

Jana looked helplessly at Mrs. Foss, but the nurse's face remained expressionless. I know she wants me to give Gorgeous to Lisa, Jana thought, even if she won't say it.

Gorgeous was looking up at her. His black eyes glistened brightly and his heart-shaped mouth smiled softly. He would make anyone feel better, Jana thought. Sighing deeply, she released her grip on Gorgeous and held him out to the nurse. "I guess she can hold him for a little while," she said reluctantly. A lump swelled in her throat as Mrs. Foss took Gorgeous out of her hands and gently placed him beside Lisa.

"His name is Gorgeous," Jana said in a voice crackling with tears. "Be very, very careful with him. Okay?"

Lisa nodded and drew Gorgeous nearer, hugging him tightly. Then she put her cheek down next to his and closed her eyes as a fluttery sigh escaped her lips. A moment later she was snoring softly.

Jana watched her sleep, thinking how sorry she felt for the little girl. It must be awful to be separated from your parents in a hospital in a strange city, and I'm glad Gorgeous made her feel better. But why can't anyone understand how much I need him myself? she thought miserably.

To Jana's amazement, Lisa slept through the rest of the morning with her arms wrapped tightly around Gorgeous. She did not open her eyes when the nurses and aides made rounds checking charts and refilling water bottles. And Lisa barely stirred when the table between the two beds was moved aside so that the telephone could be plugged into the wall. Jana glanced at the sleeping child as she picked up the phone.

"Main desk. May I help you?" asked a woman on the other end of the line.

"Yes, thank you," said Jana. "I would like to check on the condition of Randy Kirwan. He's in intensive care."

"One moment, please." The woman was gone from the line for only a few seconds. "Yes, ma'am. His condition is unchanged. Is there anything else I can help you with?"

"By 'unchanged,' do you mean he hasn't awakened yet?" Jana asked anxiously.

"I'm afraid you'll have to check with his doctor on that," said the woman. "The only information that I have is what I gave you."

"Thank you," Jana murmured. Hanging up the phone, she looked helplessly at the ceiling. "What am I going to do?" she whispered. "What *on earth* am I going to do?"

Lisa clung tenaciously to Gorgeous, refusing to give him back no matter how Jana brought up the subject, and she was still hugging him tightly when Mrs. Foss came bustling into the room after lunch and announced to Jana that she had visitors.

"Now?" asked Jana. It was too early in the day for her friends to be here. School wasn't out yet. And she had just gotten off the phone with her mother, who had called to give her the get-well messages from The Fabulous Five. "Who is it?" she asked.

Before Mrs. Foss could answer, a man and a woman appeared in the doorway. The man was tall with dark, wavy hair, and the woman was very petite with soft brown hair and big blue eyes. Jana recognized them immediately, and she drew in her breath in surprise. It was Mr. and Mrs. Kirwan, Randy's parents.

"Hi," Jana said shyly. Then she put her hand over the left side of her face, trying to hide her ugly bruises.

"Hello, Jana," said Mrs. Kirwan as the two of them came toward her. "How are you feeling?"

"That's a nasty bump," said Randy's father. "I'll bet it hurt a lot."

"It feels better now," she assured them. She tried to smile, but a question was burning in her mind. "How's Randy? Is he awake yet?"

The Kirwans exchanged guarded looks, and Mr. Kirwan put an arm around his wife's shoulder.

"No, dear," said Mrs. Kirwan. "But the doctors are very hopeful. They're convinced that he'll regain consciousness soon."

"The reason we came up to see you was to tell you

that no matter what happens, we are very proud of Randy for what he did yesterday," said Mr. Kirwan. "He cares about you very much."

"That's right," said Randy's mother. She leaned forward and tenderly brushed Jana's bruised cheek with her hand. "You mustn't blame yourself. It was just one of those terrible things that happen now and then. An accident. It was no one's fault."

"But it *was* my fault," Jana insisted. "I shouldn't have lost my temper and run away from him. And I should *never* have run into the street without looking. It was dumb! And stupid! And I'd give anything if I could make things like they were before it happened." She blinked hard to keep tears from rushing into her eyes.

"Of course you would, dear," said Randy's mother. "We all would. But it's important that you realize that everyone loses their temper now and then and says or does things they're sorry for. That still doesn't make you responsible for Randy's condition."

Jana looked away for a moment. She was puzzled. Why were Randy's parents insisting that she wasn't to blame? And how could they know how she felt? She hadn't told anyone that she believed the accident was her fault. The idea was just too awful to say out loud.

"It was sweet of you to send the card, just the

same," Mr. Kirwan assured her. "Did your mother mail it for you on her way to work this morning? It came up on the afternoon mail cart."

"What card?" Jana asked in amazement.

"This one," said Randy's mother. She opened her purse and pulled out a greeting card, which she handed to Jana. "It is from you, isn't it?"

Jana took the card and stared at it. On the front was a bouquet of roses with a bright yellow butterfly perched on one flower and the words "Get Well" printed across the top.

"I've never seen this . . ." she said as she opened it, but she stopped in midsentence when she looked inside. There was no verse, only a picture of a single red rose, and no signature. But underneath the rose and written in a delicate handwriting it said, "I'm sorry. Please forgive me."

She looked at Randy's mother in astonishment and slowly shook her head.

"Then who could have sent it?" whispered Mrs. Kirwan.

Looking flustered, Mr. Kirwan took the card from Jana's hand. "I apologize," he said. "We thought it must be from you since you were with him when the accident happened. It seemed likely that you might blame yourself." Squinting at the card again, he added, "and it certainly looks more like a girl's handwriting than a boy's."

"Oh, Jana. I'm so sorry," said Randy's mother. "I hope we didn't upset you too much. I just can't imagine who sent it, but whoever it was must feel responsible for the accident. There wasn't anyone else around when it happened, was there?"

For the hundredth time, Jana tried to bring back the memory, but she couldn't. Shaking her head she answered, "No. At least I don't think so."

"We'd better go and let her rest," said Mr. Kirwan.

His wife nodded and squeezed Jana's hand. "I know Randy will want you to visit him as soon as he's feeling better," she said. "And we'll tell him that you're going to be fine just as soon as we can talk to him."

They said good-bye and left the room. Jana watched them go with thoughts spinning wildly in her head. Whoever had sent the card to Randy believed that she had caused the accident instead of Jana. There was only one person who that could be. One person who was trying to come between Randy and Jana. A person named Laura McCall.

CHAPTER

7

A little while later Lisa was wheeled off to the X-ray room. Jana would have been glad to have the room to herself for a while except for the fact that the little girl insited on taking Gorgeous with her. When was she going to get her bear back? she wondered. Mrs. Foss was being absolutely no help in the matter, and she had been the one who had persuaded Jana to loan Lisa the bear in the first place. *For a few minutes*, she had said. "Some few minutes," Jana grumbled.

Just then she heard giggling in the hall, and she looked up hopefully. Maybe it was her friends. The sound was moving closer, but it stopped outside her door and there was only silence for a moment. Finally The Fabulous Five gathered stiffly in the doorway and peered in at her with big eyes.

"Come on in, you guys," she called out. "Haven't you ever been in a hospital before?"

The four girls grinned self-consciously and tiptoed in, standing in a cluster at the foot of the bed.

"Hi, Jana. How are you feeling?" whispered Melanie.

"Okay," said Jana, chuckling. "But you don't have to whisper."

"Doesn't your head hurt?" asked Beth. "It looks awful. Well, what I mean is . . ." Beth blushed and looked to the others for help.

"I know what you mean, silly," said Jana. "It does look awful, and it did hurt a lot for a while, but it's better now. Honest. The doctor just wants me to stay one more night for observation."

There was another awkward silence as the four girls at the foot of the bed exchanged glances. Finally Christie spoke.

"How's Randy?" she asked in a hushed voice. "We heard that he's still unconscious. Is that true?"

Jana bit her lip to stop it from quivering. She'd known they would ask about Randy, but still, she felt a stab of pain when Christie actually said the words.

"Yes," she said. "He's in the intensive care unit, and I tried to get in to see him this morning, but the nurse wouldn't let me go in."

"You're kidding," said Katie. "That's awful."

"That's not all," Jana added. "His parents stopped by to see me a little while ago, and something really strange happened. Someone sent Randy a get-well card. The handwriting looked like a girl's, and whoever sent it didn't sign their name, but they apologized for causing the accident. Mr. and Mrs. Kirwan thought I was the one who sent it."

"What!" screeched Beth.

Jana told them about her visit from the Kirwans and how they had thought she blamed herself for the accident. "They came in here to tell me that it wasn't my fault and thank me for sending the card," said Jana. "The funny thing is, I do feel responsible for the accident. If I hadn't run out in front of the car, Randy wouldn't have had to save me. But I didn't send the card. I think I know who did, though. Laura McCall."

"I agree, and there's something else you should know about Laura," said Christie. There was an ominous sound in her voice that made Jana shiver. "The four of us went up to her before school today and demanded to know what was going on between her and Randy."

"That's right," said Katie. "We told her about

what you overhead her saying to Tammy yesterday, but we didn't tell her that it was you who overheard it."

"What did she say to that?" demanded Jana.

"She just got a funny look on her face at first," said Christie. "The rest of The Fantastic Foursome were with her, and they tried to get her to walk away from us, but Laura looked so shocked that she just stood there and stared at us."

"I think it really blew her away that someone had overheard her," added Beth.

"So, what did she say?" insisted Jana.

"Get this," said Christie. "Laura said it was a secret and for us to mind our own business. Then she flipped her braid over her shoulder the way she always does when she's acting superior and walked off with her friends."

Jana frowned as she looked from one to the other. "You're kidding," she said slowly. "What kind of secret could she have about Randy?"

Melanie shook her head. "I don't know, but if you ask me, it had to be Laura who sent the card. It sounds as if she's feeling guilty."

"What about the driver? Don't forget that he's partly responsible, too," said Katie. "I mean, he had to be going pretty fast."

"Yeah," agreed Christie. "I'll bet he was speeding."

The others nodded.

Jana nodded, too. "He was probably doing a zillion miles an hour above the speed limit. I'll bet that he was going too fast to stop in time to avoid hitting Randy so he just kept on going."

"Right," said Katie. "Don't you dare blame yourself even one little bit, Jana. If it wasn't at least partly his fault, then why did he run away, and why won't he come forward now? I'd like to get my hands on him in Teen Court."

Tears blurred Jana's eyes. "He's not going to get away with it, and neither is Laura McCall. I don't know what I'm going to do, but I have to do something," she vowed.

"And we'll help you," Melanie assured her.

"The accident made the ten-o'clock news on television last night," said Christie. "And today's newspaper says Randy's a hero."

"The newspaper?" asked Jana.

Katie nodded. "We got a copy out of the vending machine in the lobby and read the article before we came up. Here. Do you want to see it?"

She held the paper out, and Jana grabbed it eagerly, scanning down page one until she found the article.

Local Teens Victims of
Hit-and-Run

One local teenager remains hospitalized in critical condition today and another is in good condition after being struck in front of Bumpers Restaurant yesterday afternoon by a car that did not stop.

Police are investigating the accident, in which they believe Randal Kirwan, 13, raced into the street and pushed Jana Morgan, 13, out of the path of a speeding car that struck him before leaving the scene. Friends and relatives praised Kirwan's actions and called him a hero. A hospital spokesman reported that he sustained both head and internal injuries and is in a coma. Morgan suffered a concussion and bumps and bruises.

Police are urging anyone with information on the driver or the car involved in the accident to come forward.

"You see," said Beth. "It says right there that he was a hero. Doesn't that make you feel proud?"

Jana nodded, thinking to herself that the newspaper also said that Randy was in a coma. Somehow the word "coma" sounded so much worse than "unconscious" or "not awake yet." Even Randy's parents hadn't used that word. People stayed in comas for ages sometimes, and *sometimes* they didn't wake up at all.

"All everybody talked about at school today is the accident," said Beth, interrupting Jana's thoughts. "So many kids were at Bumpers when it happened and heard the tires screech and the car gun its engine as it sped away."

Jana caught her breath. "Did anybody see who the driver was or get a license plate number or anything?"

Her friends shook their heads. "A policeman came to school this afternoon," said Christie. "He wanted to talk to anyone who was at Bumpers when it happened, but I don't think anybody could tell him very much. They were all inside. You don't remember anyone coming out when you two did, do you?"

Jana shook her head.

Christie sat down on the side of Jana's bed and took her hand. "You ran out of Bumpers because you were mad at Randy for sitting with Laura. Then Randy ran after you. What actually happened when you got outside? Do you remember anything?"

"Not really," Jana admitted. "He wanted me to stop and talk to him, but I couldn't. I was too upset. I just wanted to get away and think things over. The last thing I remember is starting to run across the street."

Just then Mrs. Foss stuck her head into the room. "Girls," she said kindly, "I think you'd better go now. Jana has had enough company for one day. If she gets her rest, she may be able to go home tomorrow."

Jana didn't want her friends to leave, but after they were gone, she was surprised at how their visit had tired her. She lay back, replaying their conversation and letting the new realizations sink in. They had been right. She wasn't the only one who was to blame for the accident, after all. Laura was, and so was the driver of the car.

"It's incredible," she whispered. "Randy is lying in a hospital bed two floors below so badly hurt that he's in a coma, and the two people who are the most responsible have gotten away."

CHAPTER

8

Jana was half asleep when she heard a tiny voice saying, "Gorgeous, I love you, too. I miss my mommy and daddy, but I won't be afraid as long as you're here."

Jana had napped for a little while and had only been vaguely aware of Lisa's being wheeled back into the room from X-ray. Now she perked up her ears at the sound of the little girl talking to Gorgeous.

"What did you say, Gorgeous?" asked Lisa. "Oh. Yes. I will. I promise."

Jana tried to peer out of the corner of her eye and see what was going on without Lisa's knowing it.

What was she promising, anyway? Jana wondered. Of course she knew it was only an imaginary conversation, but still!

"What did you say, Gorgeous?" Lisa asked brightly. "A secret? Okay. You can whisper it to me."

Of all the nerve! thought Jana. She turned her head and looked across at Lisa, who was propped up in bed with Gorgeous sitting on her cast. His white, plush arms were around her neck, and he looked for all the world as if he were whispering in Lisa's ear. Jana tried to fight down feelings of jealousy. After all, she told herself, he's just a stuffed bear. But the longer she looked at Lisa and Gorgeous, the angrier she got.

"Lisa, I think you'd better give Gorgeous back to me now," said Jana. "I said you could hold him for a little while, but it's been all day. I really want him back."

"No!" cried Lisa. "He's my bear. You said I could have him!"

Jana was mortified. "I didn't say you could have him, Lisa. And he's not your bear. He's mine. He's very special. My boyfriend gave him to me."

"Mine! Mine! Mine!" Lisa shrieked at the top of her lungs. Then she grabbed Gorgeous and let out a bloodcurdling scream.

"What's going on in here?" A heavyset nurse, who

had come on for the evening shift, came puffing into the room. "Are you all right, honey?" she cried, running over to Lisa.

"She's trying to steal my bear," Lisa sobbed.

The nurse was frowning when she turned to Jana. "What's this little girl talking about?" she demanded.

"It's not her bear," Jana insisted. "It's mine. I loaned it to her for a little while this morning, but she won't give it back."

"No! No! It's mine!" Lisa cried. Tears streamed down her face, and her nose was beginning to run. Jana watched in horror as Lisa buried her face in Gorgeous's soft, white middle and wiped her nose. "She's lying," Lisa said in a pouty voice. "She's trying to take him away from me."

"Nurse!" Jana begged. She threw off her covers and got stiffly out of bed, intending to grab Gorgeous away from Lisa if she had to. "She's ruining my bear. Look at that. She wiped her nose on him!" Jana shouted, pointing toward Lisa.

The nurse shot her a suspicious look.

"Well, he really is mine," Jana went on defensively, "and he's the most special bear in the world. I got him for Valentine's Day from my boyfriend, Randy Kirwan, and now Randy's in the intensive care unit in critical condition. He's even in a coma. You've got to make her give my bear back to me."

The nurse gave an exasperated sigh and looked first at Lisa and then at Jana and then back at Lisa again as if trying to decide whom to believe. As if on cue, Lisa began to moan as though her heart would break, rocking back and forth with Gorgeous in her arms.

Just then Jana heard footsteps outside the door and her mother and Pink came into the room. "Hi, sweetie," her mother said, hurrying toward her. Then she stopped and got a quizzical look on her face. "What are you doing out of bed again? I thought the doctor told you to stay put."

"Hi, Mom. Hi, Pink. Umm . . . I . . ." she began.

Mrs. Pinkerton glanced at Lisa. "Oh, I see you have a roommate," she said, smiling at the child. "Isn't that Gorgeous she's holding?"

Jana felt a flood of relief. Now she could prove to the nurse that Gorgeous really was her bear. "Yes, Mom. This is Lisa Pratt. She was in an accident, and her parents are in the hospital, too, only she can't see them yet. They're from out of state so there's no other family around to visit her."

"And you got out of bed to let her borrow Gorgeous. Oh, Jana. That's so thoughtful of you. Everybody needs somebody to hug and to hold on to, especially when they're all alone and scared."

Jana couldn't believe what she had just heard. She

started to protest again, to shout to her mother, *But Mom, that's Gorgeous. You know how special he is!* Still, the pitiful look on the little girl's face made her hesitate. Lisa's eyes were red and her blond hair was tangled, with one long strand stuck to her sweaty cheek.

Jana sank back onto the bed. Lisa is scared to death, she admitted to herself. It must be awful to be lying in a strange hospital with a broken leg and not even be able to see your parents.

She thought about how Mrs. Foss had asked her to help make Lisa feel better. Jana bit her lower lip, suddenly feeling guilty. I could have talked to her or something, but I was too busy with my own problems to pay any attention to her, she thought. I guess Lisa really does need Gorgeous more than I do right now. Just like Mom said, she thought sheepishly, she needs somebody to hug.

"It's okay if she keeps him a little longer," Jana offered, climbing back into bed. "At least until in the morning. That way she won't have to sleep all by herself."

Later, when visiting hours were over and the lights in the room had been turned out for the night, Jana tossed and turned. Now she was the one who felt all alone and frightened. What was going to happen to Randy? Was he going to wake up and be okay? Or would he die without her ever getting to see him again?

The thought made her sit straight up in bed. What's the matter with everybody! she wanted to shout. Why aren't the doctors doing anything to help Randy? And what about the police? Why haven't they found the hit-and-run driver and put him in jail? And what about Laura McCall? She's the biggest villain of all. If it hadn't been for her, there never would have been an accident in the first place.

Jana looked helplessly around the darkened room until her gaze fell on Lisa, who was snuggled up against Gorgeous, snoring and whimpering ever so softly in her sleep. Jana was flooded with feelings of sympathy. As badly as she hated to admit it to herself, she knew that Lisa needed the bear.

"But what about me?" she whispered. "I'm scared, too."

CHAPTER

9

Jana was released from the hospital the next morning. But as much as she longed to be at home, away from the noisy halls and awful food and back where she could have some privacy and sleep in her own bed, when she walked out through the lobby, there was a lump in her throat. Randy was still there in a deep sleep and barely clinging to life. She had brushed tears from her eyes when her mother told her that the morning report on Randy's condition was just the same as it had been the day before. No change.

Also left behind was Gorgeous. Jana had tried to

think of another way to ask Lisa to give him back, but the sight of the sad little girl clutching the bear and staring at her with anxious eyes had made it impossible to do. Instead she had taken Mrs. Foss aside and explained the situation. The nurse had promised to get Gorgeous back for Jana before Lisa left the hospital. Then she put her arms around Jana and hugged her, saying, "It's wonderful of you to let her keep him so long. She really needs him, you know." Jana had nodded silently and turned away before Mrs. Foss could see the tears in her eyes.

When she got home, she found a long list of messages beside the telephone. In addition to The Fabulous Five, tons of her friends had called. Alexis Duvall, Kim Baxter, Sara Sawyer, and Lisa Snow, all old friends from Mark Twain Elementary, had sent get-well wishes. Even Taffy Sinclair had called. So had Whitney Larkin and Shawnie Pendergast. Some boys had called, too. Curtis Trowbridge had called twice. Joel Murphy, Keith Masterson, Scott Daly, and Shane Arrington had left messages, and Shane had told her mother that Igor, his pet iguana, sent a special get-well wish. Jana couldn't help chuckling about that.

Near the bottom of the list of names was Funny Hawthorne's. Jana drummed her fingers on the telephone and wondered if she should call Funny back right away. Funny was the only one who might be able to clear up the mystery about Laura McCall. What was the secret she was keeping about Randy Kirwan? And why had she sent the card to Randy saying she was sorry if she wasn't feeling guilty about the accident? But Funny was also one of Laura's best friends. She might feel as if she were betraying that friendship if she answered Jana's questions. But Funny's my friend, too, Jana thought stubbornly. There was no use putting it off, she decided. She had to know about Laura.

Funny was her usual bright and cheerful self when she answered the phone. "Hello," she sang. "Hawthorne residence."

"Hi, Funny. This is Jana."

"Wow! Jana! I've been so worried about you. How are you feeling? Are you still in the hospital?"

"Whoa," said Jana with a chuckle. "Slow down. I'm feeling a lot better, and no, I'm not still in the hospital. The doctor let me come home a little while ago."

"Terrific. Can you have company? I'd love to come over and see you if it's okay."

Jana sighed. "Mom says I have to wait until tomorrow to have company, but there is something I wanted to talk to you about."

"Sure. Fire away," said Funny.

Jana bit her lower lip, trying to choose her words carefully. "It's about Laura," she said finally, "and

Randy Kirwan." For the next couple of minutes she explained to Funny about what she had overheard Laura saying to Tammy and about seeing Laura and Randy sitting together in Bumpers just before the accident. She wanted to shout that it had all been Laura's fault, but she didn't. Instead she said, "If you know what's going on between them, please tell me. I *have* to know."

"I wish I did know, but I don't," said Funny. "Honest. Laura talks to Tammy and Melissa a lot more than to me lately. I guess it's because you and I are friends. I have seen her talking to Randy several times lately, though, and I heard what your friends said to her before school yesterday morning. But still, I can't imagine that anything is going on between them. As far as I know, she still has a crush on Shane Arrington. She's been after him since sixth grade."

"There's something else," said Jana. "Somebody sent Randy a get-well card and didn't sign it. Instead, they wrote 'I'm sorry. Please forgive me' on it. I think the person who sent it feels responsible for the accident. I also think it was Laura McCall."

Funny didn't say anything for a moment. When she did, the sparkle was gone from her voice. "Gosh. I'll see what I can find out. I'm not sure she'll tell me anything, but I promise to try. I'll call you back as soon as I can."

"Thanks, Funny," said Jana. "I know it's not going to be easy. You're a real friend."

Jana waited for the rest of the day for Funny to call back, but she didn't. Several of her other friends did, though, including all of The Fabulous Five, and they promised to visit her on Sunday afternoon.

"How about if I order out some pizza for supper?" offered Pink later in the afternoon. "We need to celebrate your homecoming."

"Pizza?" said Jana, feeling pleasantly surprised. Pink always got her a deep-dish, pepperoni, green pepper, and mushroom pizza on Saturday night before he and her mom went bowling. It was her absolute favorite food in the world. "Great. Are you guys going bowling?"

"No way," Pink assured her. "We plan to spend the evening with you. The pizza's just a little something extra."

But when the pizza was delivered and the three of them sat down to eat it, Jana couldn't take a bite. The instant she saw it sitting there on the kitchen table in the box from Mama Mia's Pizzeria she remembered that it was Randy's favorite, too.

Her mom and Pink were looking at her with quizzical expressions. She knew she should at least take one bite to show them she appreciated their thoughtfulness, but she was sure she would never be able to swallow it around the lump in her throat.

Jana slowly pushed her chair away from the table and stood up. "I guess I'm just not very hungry right now," she said. "I'm sorry. Save a couple of slices for me, and I'll warm them in the microwave later. Okay?"

Pink and her mother exchanged worried glances, and then Mrs. Pinkerton said, "Of course, honey. I'm sure you aren't feeling like your old self yet. Why don't you watch some television for a little while and try to rest?"

Pink nodded sympathetically, and Jana told them thank you with her eyes as she went into the living room and sank onto the sofa. Picking up the remote control, she aimed it at the set and punched the on button, not caring what she watched. Her heart was too heavy with worry over Randy.

The news was on, and Marge Whitworth, the local anchorwoman, was talking about a senator in Washington, D.C., who had suffered a heart attack at his desk.

"And now for local news," said Ms. Whitworth. "Police are continuing to investigate the hit-and-run accident Thursday, which slightly injured one teenager and left a second in critical condition."

Jana's heart almost stopped, and she leapt off the sofa and landed on her knees just inches from the set, remembering too late how stiff and sore she was from the accident.

"Authorities say that they have pieced together enough information from witnesses to get a partial description of the car. It was a black or dark blue, late-model, two-door sedan. The license plate number began with three seven and ended with nine. Anyone with additional information is asked to contact the police department as soon as possible."

"Oh, my gosh!" Jana shouted.

"What was that about the accident?" asked Pink, who was coming into the room carrying a slice of pizza. Her mother was right behind him. "Your mom and I thought we heard something about it on the television."

"Witnesses saw the car and got part of the license number! Now maybe they can find the driver and put him in jail!" The words gushed out of Jana almost faster than she could move her lips. Her eyes narrowed. "I just hope he hasn't skipped town," she grumbled. "He deserves to be punished for what he did."

"I'm sure they'll find him, sweetheart," her mother said. "They can run the partial license plate number through the computer at the department of motor vehicles and check out every car in the state that matches. It may take a while, but they'll find him. Now why don't you try to eat something? This pizza is delicious. It won't taste nearly as good warmed over."

Jana followed her mother and Pink back into the kitchen like a robot and ate three slices of pizza without tasting any of it. All she could think about was the hit-and-run driver and how the police were closing in on him at that very moment. She smiled to herself. Someone was finally doing something, and for the first time since the accident, there was something to get her hopes up for.

CHAPTER

10

A little later Funny called. "You're not going to believe this," she said in an excited voice.

"What? Tell me," Jana insisted. She feared the worst, but she had to know.

"Okay. I'll start at the beginning. I called Laura and said that I really didn't understand what The Fabulous Five were talking about yesterday when they asked her what was going on between her and Randy Kirwan. At first, she insisted that it was nothing. She said it was all a big mistake, but I kept pushing, and finally she told me the whole story."

"So, what did she say?" Jana urged.

"Are you sitting down?"

"Yes. Shoot," said Jana.

"Okay. Laura's still crazy about Shane Arrington."

"What!" cried Jana.

"Sure," said Funny. "You remember, don't you? I told you she had a crush on him in sixth grade. Anyway, Laura's desperate to get him to ask her out, but she's heard some rumors that he doesn't like her anymore. It's her attitude. He thinks she's a snob. Actually, he likes Melanie a lot better because she's sweet and friendly to everybody."

"So, what does that have to do with Randy? That's who I heard her talking about. Not Shane."

"This is where it starts getting unbelievable," said Funny with a laugh. "Laura asked Randy to bring her name up when he's around Shane and then talk her up. You know, improve her image. She thought if Randy could impress Shane with how great she was, Shane would ask her out."

"Do you mean she actually asked Randy to do a thing like that?" Jana shouted into the phone. It was too incredible to be true.

"She was a little more subtle than that," Funny said. "She just asked him to do her a favor and say nice things about her to Shane once in a while."

"No wonder Randy was laughing when I saw them together," Jana muttered.

"What did you say?"

"Nothing," said Jana. "But I'm still not convinced. If everything was so innocent, then why did she send the get-well card to Randy, and why did she tell Tammy that she wanted Randy to confess to me about the two of them? Explain that, if you can."

"She said that she definitely did not send the card. She also said that she was trying to prevent the exact thing that happened—your getting mad. She was afraid that if you saw her talking to Randy a lot, you'd start saying bad things about her that would get back to Shane. She thought that if Randy told you he was doing her some kind of favor and that's why he was talking to her so much, then you'd keep quiet about her."

"And Shane would listen to Randy, fall madly in love with her, and then everybody would live happily ever after. Is that the idea?" asked Jana.

"You've got it," said Funny. "Although what she wanted Randy to tell you was that they were doing a school project together—not that he was helping her with her love life."

"Oh, Funny. That's hilarious. What some people won't do for romance," chuckled Jana. "Actually, she and Melanie ought to get together and compare notes on how to attract boys."

"You're right. It is pretty crazy," conceded Funny. "But I do believe her. You'll have to admit that you were wrong about her this one time."

Jana sighed, feeling as deflated as a balloon with a hole in it. She had been so sure that Laura was a villain, had even *wanted* to believe it. But now she was forced to face the truth.

"Oh, all right. I was wrong. I can't really blame her for the accident when I misinterpreted what was going on, I guess. I owe Randy an apology, too. I should have known that I could trust him. Oh, Funny. If I'd only remembered that and trusted him on Thursday, the accident would never have happened! How could I have been so stupid?"

"You weren't stupid. You were just human," Funny said gently. "Randy's pretty special. Nobody can blame you for wanting to hang on to him. Besides, accidents are accidents. Nobody means for them to happen."

"Thanks, Funny, but I still feel pretty horrible. I just hope they get the hit-and-run driver." She told Funny what she had heard on television earlier about the partial description of the car and some of the numbers on the license plate. "That guy belongs behind bars. It may have been an accident, but you can't say *he* wasn't to blame."

"Yeah," said Funny. "I guess you're right about him. If he wasn't guilty, he would have stayed at the scene and tried to help you and Randy."

Before they hung up, Funny said, "So promise me that you won't do anything to let Laura know what

I've just told you. She'd kill me if she knew I told you all that. Now that you and I are friends, she doesn't trust me very much anyway."

"O-*kay*," Jana said grudgingly.

"Thanks," said Funny.

"There's just one thing," added Jana. "Can I tell The Fabulous Five if I swear them to secrecy? I've just *got* to tell someone."

"Oh, all right," said Funny. "But make *sure* they keep it a secret."

Jana called each of her four friends the instant Funny and she hung up, saving Melanie for last.

"What!" shrieked Melanie when she had heard the whole story. "How can you call Laura innocent when she's scheming to get Shane away from me?"

"Okay, so she's not exactly innocent," Jana conceded. "At least she's your problem now, instead of mine."

"Well, maybe she's not so much of a problem if Shane is saying that he likes me better than her," Melanie said gleefully.

"That reminds me. How's your checklist for boyfriends coming along?" asked Jana.

"Who needs it? I'm going to throw it away and just concentrate on Shane," said Melanie in a breathless voice. "I can't let Laura McCall take him away from me."

Later, when she was getting ready for bed, Jana

heard the phone ring again. A few minutes later her mother knocked on her door.

"Come in," called Jana.

"It was the police. They've found the hit-and-run driver," Mrs. Pinkerton said. "They were able to identify the car through the description and the partial license plate number just the way we thought."

"Terrific!" shouted Jana, thrusting a fist into the air. "Did they get the driver? Is he in jail?"

"It isn't a he," her mother said quietly. "It's a she. Her name is Erica Fleming, and she's sixteen. She said she had only had her driver's license for three days when the accident happened, and she left the scene because she panicked, thinking no one would believe her side of the story."

Jana wrinkled her nose. "Her side of the story? What's to believe? She ran down Randy, didn't she?"

Mrs. Pinkerton looked away for a moment. "She says that she was driving along staying well below the speed limit when you raced into the street no more than six feet in front of her car. There was no way for her to stop in time. She's also the one who sent the get-well card to Randy. She's really upset about the accident."

Jana closed her eyes and let her breath out slowly. She was too stunned to speak. She had been so sure. So positive that the hit-and-run driver was the real person who was responsible for Randy's condition.

Somehow she had even believed that once the driver was found and put in jail, everything would get better. Randy would wake up, and things would be the way they had been before.

But now she knew better. The driver had been a scared teenager who couldn't stop. It was an accident. Nobody's fault, and at the same time, everybody's fault. Laura's fault for causing Jana to lose her temper, and yet it wasn't Laura's fault. The driver's fault for not stopping, and yet it wasn't the driver's fault. And her own fault for running into the street without looking, and yet not totally her fault, either.

"What's going to happen to Erica Fleming?" asked Jana.

"I imagine her driver's license will be suspended right away," said her mother. "After that, what happens will be up to a judge."

Jana cringed. "Even though the accident wasn't her fault?"

Mrs. Pinkerton nodded. "Being a licensed driver carries a lot of responsibility. It's still against the law to leave the scene of an accident even if the accident wasn't your fault."

Jana thought about that for a moment. Poor Erica Fleming, she thought. I've been hating her and wanting her in jail ever since the accident, but now I know it wasn't really her fault. Because I ran out in front of her car, she's in trouble. It isn't fair.

"I know you're feeling awfully confused right now," her mother said gently. "You want someone to blame, and you want some way to make things the way they were before the accident happened."

Jana blinked at her mother, amazed that she had read her mind.

"But no one can ever change the past," said her mother. "And many times there's no one to blame. All you can do in a situation like this is go forward and try your best to make things better."

"But *how*?" Jana begged. "What can I do?"

Mrs. Pinkerton shook her head and smiled gently. "I don't know, Jana. You'll have to find out for yourself, but if you look hard enough, I'm sure you'll find a way."

CHAPTER

11

"My friends are going to throw up when they see my face," Jana grumbled the next afternoon as she plopped down on the sofa to wait for The Fabulous Five to arrive.

"They've already seen it," her mother reminded her. "They came to visit you in the hospital. Remember?"

"But they haven't seen it since the bruises turned yellow," said Jana. The scrapes had almost disappeared from her hands and the knot on her forehead had gone down, but the bruises that had been angry and purple right after the accident had now turned a

sickly yellowish color. Jana had spent twenty minutes trying to cover them up with her mother's liq-
uid makeup before giving up in disgust. "And my
hair looks like something a cat coughed up," she
added in a pouty voice.

Pink looked at her from over the top of his newspaper. "Hey, come on, Jana. Don't be so down on
yourself."

Jana sighed loudly. "I'm just depressed," she conceded. "This is Sunday, and the accident happened
on Thursday, and the doctors haven't done anything
to get Randy to wake up. How long is it going to
take?"

"I'm sure the doctors are doing everything they
can, sweetheart," said her mother.

Jana jumped up and began pacing the floor. Another canned answer. That was all she ever got from
anybody, she thought angrily. It was so frustrating.
Her mother kept assuring her that everyone was
doing all they could. The lady who gave out patient
information at the hospital kept saying that Randy's
condition hadn't changed. But nobody could explain
what was really happening or when he was going to
get better. She was beginning to think that she
couldn't stand it any longer. "There has to be *something* to do, but I can't think of anything that will
help," she said, stopping in front of her mother and
looking at her imploringly.

Her mother gave her a helpless shrug. "I know, sweetheart, but you just have to face the fact that all you can do for the moment is wait. The doctors *are* doing all they can. You just have to be patient and keep your hopes up."

Jana frowned at her mother. Of course she was keeping her hopes up. Why did parents always say things like that? But before she could think of an appropriate response the doorbell rang. "I'll get it. It's probably my friends," she mumbled, and scurried to the door, glad to have the conversation at an end.

Katie, Christie, Beth, and Melanie were clustered in the hallway outside her apartment. They were all smiles when she opened the door.

"I'm so glad you're home from the hospital," cried Beth, rushing forward and hugging her.

"Ooooh. I'll bet that still hurts," said Melanie, wrinkling her nose and gently touching Jana's forehead with a finger.

"I still can't believe it happened," said Katie, shaking her head in amazement. "I mean, you read about these kind of accidents in the paper, but you never think they'll happen to anyone you know."

The girls crowded into the apartment and said hi to Pink and Jana's mother as they headed for Jana's room. She was just about to close the door when she heard Pink call her name.

"What?" she called back, sticking her head out.

"Need a mop?" asked Pink.

"A mop?" she asked. "Why would I need a mop?"

"You said your friends would throw up," he teased.

Jana couldn't help laughing. Pink loved to tease her, and he could usually make her see the funny side of a bad situation. She tossed him a grateful smile and pulled her head back into the room, but when she turned to her friends, her black mood was back again. It didn't improve when she told them about the hit-and-run driver, even though she knew deep down that it hadn't really been the girl's fault.

"Have you checked on Randy's condition today?" asked Melanie, who had sprawled across Jana's bed while the others had arranged themselves in various spots on the floor.

Jana nodded. "A little while ago. It's the same old story. No change. I could just scream. That woman sounds like a broken record."

"I'm sure the doctors are doing everything they can," offered Christie.

Jana bristled. "You sound just like my mother." Making a face, she mocked her mother's voice: "You have to be patient and keep your hopes up." Then she let out a sigh of exasperation and said, "How can I be patient and keep my hopes up when as far as I can tell nobody is *doing* anything? Why doesn't the hospital call in a specialist or something? There has to be *somebody* who knows what to do!"

Her friends looked embarrassed, and no one said anything. Tears of frustration welled in Jana's eyes, and she looked pleadingly at her friends and said, "Mom says that since there's no way to make things like they were before and nobody to blame, I can only try to find a way to make things better. But how?"

No one had an answer for that.

"If only they would let me in to see him," said Jana.

"What good would that do?" asked Beth, putting a sympathetic arm around Jana. "Let's face it. If the doctors can't wake him up, how could you? He's just lying there, sleeping."

Jana didn't answer for a moment. She was staring out into space and thinking over Beth's words about how Randy was just lying there sleeping. She could visualize him lying on a beautiful canopy bed. He was sleeping so peacefully, and he looked so handsome that her eyes filled with tears. The vision widened, and she could see that the beautiful canopy bed was in a forest. Sunbeams crisscrossed the air, and all around him birds sang and woodland creatures stopped to look at him.

Suddenly Jana recognized the scene. She had seen it in her mind hundreds of times before, and a crazy idea popped into her head. It was so crazy that she was almost afraid to say it out loud. Her friends would think she had completely flipped out, but maybe this was it—the something that she could do to make Randy better.

"Do you remember the story of Sleeping Beauty?" she asked.

Everyone nodded.

"Well, don't you see? Randy is like Sleeping Beauty!" she said as excitement rose in her voice. "Everybody always thought that was just a silly fairy tale, but it wasn't. It can come true for Randy. I know it can."

"Sure, sure, only he's Sleeping Handsome. Is that it?" said Katie, making a face. "Don't tell me you're the beautiful princess, and all you have to do is kiss him and he'll wake up. Come on, Jana. Get real! The day you do that, I'll go kiss a frog."

"I didn't mean kiss him, silly. I'll talk to him and tell him how much I want him to wake up. I've read that people in comas can sometimes hear what other people say to them. If I tell him how much I care about him, and how sorry I am about the accident, maybe he'll hear me and want to wake up so badly that he will. And then I'll kiss him," she added, blushing.

"Oh, Jana!" Melanie groaned ecstatically. "That's the most romantic thing I ever heard!"

"Hmmm," mused Katie, slowly nodding her head. "I read that somewhere, too. You know, I hate to admit it, but it just might work. In fact," she added, with a sly grin, "I may have to kiss a frog, after all."

"Do you think you can get in to see him?" asked Christie.

"I don't know," admitted Jana. "When I went to the intensive care unit before, the nurse threatened to call security if I didn't leave. I'll have to think of another way."

"Maybe if you called Randy's parents and asked them, they would give you permission," offered Katie.

"It's worth a try," said Jana. She went to the phone and dialed the Kirwans' number, half afraid that no one would answer. His parents were probably at the hospital.

"Hello," said a woman's voice. It was Mrs. Kirwan.

"Hi, Mrs. Kirwan. This is Jana." Suddenly she didn't know what to say next. Sleeping Beauty? Sleeping Handsome? It wouldn't be an easy thing to explain.

"Yes, Jana?" said Mrs. Kirwan. Her voice sounded tired.

"I'm sorry to bother you, but I was wondering if you could give me permission to visit Randy at the hospital. You see, I have this idea . . ." she paused, searching for the right words. "Well, it's sort of like Sleeping Beauty. You know. The prince kissed her and woke her up. Well, I was thinking that if Randy could hear me when I talked to him, maybe I could convince him to wake up, too." Jana screwed up her face in frustration. "Does that make any sense?"

"Yes, Jana," said Mrs. Kirwan, sounding pleasantly surprised. "That makes a lot of sense, and I think it's a beautiful idea. Of course you can see Randy. In fact, I'll take you with me when I go back to the hospital to relieve Mr. Kirwan. We're taking turns so that someone can be with Randy all the time. I'll drive by and get you in about an hour."

"Oh, thank you, Mrs. Kirwan. Thank you *so* much," Jana murmured. "I'll be watching for you."

As she hung up the phone, she whispered to herself, "Oh, please, I want so badly to do something to help. Please let this work!"

CHAPTER

12

*T*he ride to the hospital was made in silence. After greeting Jana and saying how glad she was that Jana was coming along, Mrs. Kirwan lapsed into thoughts of her own as she drove through the dark streets. Jana sat beside her in the front seat and tried not to fidget, but the closer they got to the hospital, the more nervous she became. Had it been a crazy idea, after all? If the doctors couldn't wake Randy with all their medical skill, how could she possibly hope to do it by acting out a fairy tale?

When they reached the intensive care unit on the second floor, Jana was relieved to see that the red-haired nurse who had sent her away before was not on duty tonight. Instead, a pleasant-looking gray-haired woman looked up from her desk in the nurses' station and gave them a smile.

"Any change?" Mrs. Kirwan asked hopefully.

"I'm afraid not," said the nurse. Then looking at Jana, she said, "Hello, dear. Are you Randy's sister?"

Jana shook her head. "I'm a friend," she murmured, thinking how shocked the nurse would be if she added that she was the princess who was going into the enchanted forest to awaken Sleeping Handsome. The thought made her more jittery than ever.

The nurse smiled knowingly. "I'll bet you're a special friend. Go right on in."

Jana's heart was pounding when she stepped into Randy's room. Her eyes were immediately drawn to the electronic monitors and dials on the wall above the bed. Blips on a long, thin line recorded his heartbeat. Other machines hummed and dials moved as the big machines kept track of Randy's vital signs.

Mr. Kirwan met them just inside the door. He looked tired, but he smiled when he saw her. "Hello, Jana," he said. "What a pleasant surprise."

Jana could only nod because as her eyes adjusted to the dim light she could see Randy lying on a bed behind a screen with the covers pulled up around him. He lay very still with his eyes closed, but he didn't look anything at all like the Sleeping Handsome of her dreams. The top of his head was wound with bandages like a mummy, and an intravenous drip bottle hung upside down on a stand beside the bed and was connected to his arm by a long, thin tube.

Behind her, Jana could hear Mrs. Kirwan explaining to Randy's father why she was there. She couldn't join in the conversation. She could only stare at Randy and say a silent prayer that she could help.

"There's a chair beside the bed. Go ahead. Sit down," Mr. Kirwan urged.

Mrs. Kirwan nodded. "We'll leave the room for a few minutes so that you can have some privacy," she said. Then, seeing Jana's hesitation, she added, "We'll be right outside if you need us."

When they had gone, Jana turned back to Randy. She felt as if her heart would break. The still, sleeping form looked so different from the lively, smiling Randy she knew so well that she wanted to shout, "That's not him!" and run out of the room. Instead, she took a deep breath and tiptoed closer.

"Randy," she whispered. "It's Jana. Can you hear me?"

There was no response. He didn't move even so much as a fraction of an inch, and although she bent closer to listen, he didn't make a sound, either.

She eased into the chair. The monitors hung over-head like vultures as she struggled to regain her courage. It was like being in the middle of a night-mare. I have to go through with this, she thought desparately. I have to at least *try*.

"Randy," she said again. This time her voice was a little stronger. "I got permission to visit you because I read somewhere that some people who are in a . . . who are asleep . . . can hear what other people say to them. I hope you can hear me because I want to tell you some things."

Leaning back, she sighed deeply before she went on. This wasn't so hard, after all. All she had to do was talk to him the way she would if he were awake.

"First, I want to tell you that I'm sorry I didn't trust you. I know now that I was mistaken about Laura McCall. I should have known that you would try to help her if she needed it. I wish I could go back to that day and start all over. I wouldn't listen in on her conversation with Tammy, much less jump to conclusions about what she said. Also, I wouldn't get mad when I saw you talking to her at Bumpers, and I definitely would not run away from you and straight into the path of a car. Oh, Randy, you were such a hero to save me, but I'd much rather have you awake again."

She paused. There was so much more she wanted to say, but would he really be able to hear?

"Second, I wish I hadn't tried so hard to find someone to take the blame for the accident. Especially Erica Fleming, the girl who was driving the car. It wasn't fair. She couldn't stop, and she was just as scared as I was. Maybe more.

"Most of all, I just want you to know how much I love you. Please don't die. If you can hear me, please wake up so that things can be the way they were before."

Still Randy slept. Jana's eyes filled with tears of defeat as she sat watching him. Why didn't he open his eyes? Or at least move one finger? Or make a tiny sound? Or do something to let her know that he had heard her?

She sat there for a few more minutes, watching and waiting and hoping, but nothing changed. The lines on the monitors continued their quick movements across the screens, and the needles in the dials registered their numbers. Her hope was rapidly fading away. Finally, she looked at him sadly and said, "I guess I'd better go now so that your parents can come back in."

Standing up, Jana started to turn away, but something stopped her. She knew down deep that there was one more thing she had to do. Bending over Randy, she kissed him gently on the cheek and said softly, "Wake up, Sleeping Handsome."

To her astonishment his eyelids fluttered. Jana

gasped and stepped back, catching her balance on the chair. *"He heard me,"* she whispered incredulously. Was he waking up? Had the fairy tale worked?

But slowly his eyes stopped fluttering, and he went on sleeping as peacefully as before. Jana stared at him for an instant and then shook her head defiantly.

"He heard me," she said out loud for a second time. Her heart pounded inside her chest like a trapped bird. *"He isn't awake yet, but he HEARD ME!"*

Spinning around, she raced out of the room to find Randy's parents.

CHAPTER

13

"*M*r. and Mrs. Kirwan! Come quickly!" Jana shouted. "He heard me! I know he did!"

Randy's parents were sitting in a small lounge area near the door to their son's room. At the sound of Jana's voice, they both looked startled for an instant and then jumped to their feet, spilling magazines out of their laps and onto the floor.

"What happened?" gasped Mr. Kirwan.

"Is he awake?" cried his mother as both of them dashed toward Jana.

The nurse, who had been sitting peacefully at her desk, went into action, also. She flipped the switch

on her intercom and spoke rapidly into the micro-
phone. "Dr. Garza. Calling Dr. Garza. Please come
to the second floor ICU."

Jana led the Kirwans and the nurse into the dimly
lit room where Randy lay, but his eyes were closed,
and he looked as peacefully asleep as ever. The com-
motion that had begun in the hall soon died away as
the little group gathered beside his bed, and all Jana
could hear over the hum of the monitors was the
sound of anxious breathing.

Before her eyes could adjust, Dr. Garza rushed in
and hurried to Randy's side. After the nurse had
filled him in on what had happened, he said, "Please
stand back for a moment, everyone. I'd like to exam-
ine the patient."

Obediently, all of them except the nurse moved
away from the bed to allow the doctor plenty of
room. Jana held her breath. Randy *had* heard her.
She was positive. "His eyes fluttered," she whispered. "I know he'll wake up."

When Dr. Garza had finished his examination he
motioned them back to the bedside. "Now, miss,
will you tell me exactly what happened when you
thought he heard you?"

"He did hear me," Jana insisted.

The doctor nodded patiently and said, "Please go
on."

Jana hesitated. Do I have to tell him the whole

story? she wondered. All the stuff about Sleeping Handsome and the kiss? "Well," she began slowly, "I read somewhere that people in comas can sometimes hear what people say to them so I just came in and started talking."

"What did you say to him?" asked Dr. Garza. "You don't have to tell me the exact words—just what kinds of things you talked about."

Jana drew in a deep breath. "I told him how sorry I was about the accident and that I shouldn't have gotten mad at him and run into the street in front of a car. I also said I wanted him to wake up so that things could be the way they were before."

Dr. Garza nodded slowly, as if he was thinking it over carefully. "And were you sitting in the chair when his eyes fluttered? Or standing by the bed? And were you speaking? If you can be very specific about that moment, I'd appreciate it."

Oh, no, she thought. This was what she had dreaded. All four adults were staring at her now, waiting for her answer.

"Well . . ." she began. "Actually what happened was . . . I kissed him on the cheek and said, 'Wake up, Sleeping Handsome.'" Jana dropped her eyes as she felt color seeping into her face. They would think she was crazy, or at the very least, *boy* crazy.

"Oh, Jana. That's lovely," said Mrs. Kirwan, and

when Jana looked at her, she could see that Randy's mother was misty-eyed.

Dr. Garza cleared his throat and took charge again. "It's very possible that he did hear you and responded to you emotionally," he said, looking straight at Jana. "I'd say it's a very good sign, and I'd like to recommend that you visit Randy as often as you like, with Mr. and Mrs. Kirwan's approval, of course."

Jana stared at Dr. Garza, only vaguely aware that Randy's parents were insisting that she spend all the time at their son's bedside that she could and that Dr. Garza was cautioning all of them to remember that although this was a good sign, they shouldn't get their hopes up too high. She knew all that was going on around her, but her thoughts were on Randy and the moment his eyes had almost opened. She had done something. She had actually done something that might help him wake up, and she wanted to jump up and down and shout with joy.

For the next few days Jana divided her time between school during the day and the hospital in the evening. At school, she was the center of attention as everyone wanted to ask her how she felt and if she had news of Randy. Even Laura McCall stopped her in the hall between classes on Monday morning.

"I'm really sorry about the accident," Laura said. Her eyes were downcast and she spoke barely above a whisper. "Funny said that you were upset about Randy's spending so much time with me, and that's why you ran into the street. I never meant for anything so awful to happen. I was just asking him to do me a favor. Honest. That's all it was."

Jana looked at Laura thoughtfully. She had never seen Laura look so genuinely sorry. "I guess I just misunderstood," said Jana, knowing that she didn't dare betray Funny's confidence.

The biggest surprise came in the cafeteria at noon when the cheerleading squad went from table to table, pinning small bows made of the red and gold school colors on everyone and saying that they were for Randy.

Tears of gratitude welled in Jana's eyes as Melanie pinned a ribbon on her and said, "All the cheerleaders met at my house last night to make them. We wanted to do *something*."

Jana nodded, afraid her voice would crack with emotion if she tried to speak. It had seemed right after the accident that nobody was doing anything to help Randy, but now lots of people were finding things to do.

At the hospital that evening she told him about the red and gold bows. "Everybody in school is wearing one. Even the teachers and Mr. Bell, and someone said the custodian, Mr. Bartosik, had on two. Isn't that terrific?"

If Randy heard, he gave no sign. Jana sighed, touching the small bow pinned to her blouse, and went on talking softly.

"Lots of kids sent messages, too. Scott and Mark said to hang in there. Clarence said not to flirt with the nurses. Joel and Keith said to let them know as soon as you can have visitors. Oh, yes, Shane wants to come to see you, too, and he said he hopes they'll let him bring in Igor."

"Jana, it's time to go now."

Jana looked up at the sound of Mrs. Kirwan's voice. It was hard to believe that it was time to go already. It seemed that she had just gotten there, but Mr. Kirwan had arrived for his turn at Randy's bedside, and he smiled at her as he took off his coat. "Any changes?" he asked.

"No," murmured Jana. She didn't try to hide her disappointment. Randy hadn't seemed to hear a single word she had said. In fact, he seemed as deeply asleep as he had before.

"Mrs. Kirwan and I will be in the hall when you're ready to go," he said.

Jana nodded and turned back toward Randy, dreading to say good-bye. And yet, he looked so peaceful lying there. She glanced toward the glass-topped doors that led into the hallway to be sure no one was peering in, and then she bent toward Randy and softly kissed his cheek. "Good night, Sleeping Handsome," she whispered. She waited for his eyes to open. At least to flutter as they had before. But this time nothing happened, and with a heavy heart, she turned and headed for the door.

CHAPTER

14

The next afternoon Jana left school loaded down with gifts for Randy. His English class had made a banner that was ten feet long and signed by everyone. The football team had autographed a football for him, and students from all three grades had given her get-well cards to take to him.

As she stepped into the hospital lobby with Mrs. Kirwan, she felt a stab of regret that she had nothing special for him herself. It wasn't that she hadn't tried to think of something to bring. A card had seemed too impersonal. A note, too personal until she could be sure that he would be the only one to read it.

Flowers? What good would they be until he woke up and could smell them? There was nothing. Absolutely nothing, and she gathered her frustration into the end of her finger and punched the elevator button as hard as she could.

"Oh, Jana," said Mrs. Kirwan as the doors opened and several people got out. "Would you go on up without me, dear? I see a neighbor sitting in the lounge, and I want to speak to her for a moment. I won't be long."

Jana nodded and boarded alone. She started to direct the elevator to the second floor but changed her mind, touching the button for the fourth floor instead. An idea had just occurred to her. Maybe there was something that she could take to Randy, after all.

A wave of emotion swept over her as she stepped into the familiar corridor. She had been discharged days ago, but still the sights and smells brought a rush of tears into her eyes. It was here she had awakened after the accident and learned of Randy's coma.

As she moved toward the room she had shared with Lisa, Mrs. Foss stepped out of another room and stopped, looking at her with both pleasure and surprise. "Jana. How good to see you," she said. "How are you feeling?"

"Oh, I'm fine now," Jana assured her.

Mrs. Foss cocked her head to one side and studied Jana's face. "Even your bruises are almost gone. See? We do good work here at this hospital." Then she threw back her head and laughed heartily. "So, what brings you up to see us?"

Jana hesitated. Maybe it was too soon to mention the real reason, so instead she said, "I came to see Randy, and I thought I'd stop by and check on Lisa."

Mrs. Foss's face lit up, making Jana feel even more guilty over her deception. "She's doing beautifully, the little imp. We're having a devil of a time keeping her in bed—in spite of her cast. And she doesn't have a roommate since you left, so she rings her call button every fifteen minutes for company. I don't know what she'll do when she gets home, though. She's going to be in that cast for a long time. Come on. She'll love seeing you."

Jana followed the nurse down the hall. "Look, Lisa. You have company," she said as they entered the hospital room.

"Jana! Jana!" the little girl cried happily. "Did you come to see me and Gorgeous?"

Jana tried to keep the smile on her face as she glanced at Gorgeous tucked into the covers beside Lisa, arms extended as if waiting for a hug and a gentle smile on his heart-shaped mouth. It was all she could do to keep from grabbing him and burying her face in his soft body as she had done so many times before. She longed to tell him about her fairy-tale attempt to wake Randy from his coma and to let the tears that were gathering in her eyes spill onto his soft fur.

"Want to sign my cast?" Lisa threw back the sheet to display the long white cast covered with names written in every color of the rainbow. "Here. You can put your name next to where Gorgeous wrote his."

Puzzled, Jana blinked at a large pink heart with Gorgeous written neatly inside.

"He wrote that while she was asleep," said Mrs. Foss, winking at Jana.

Jana couldn't help smiling. "Sure," she said. "I'd like to sign next to Gorgeous." She chose a green marker out of a cup of multicolored pens and wrote her name with a flourish. "There. How's that?"

"Well, I have to get back to work," said Mrs. Foss. "You two girls have a nice visit."

Jana watched her go, wishing she had had time to speak to her privately about Gorgeous. I *can't* let Lisa keep him any longer, Jana thought. Randy needs him. But how am I going to get him back?

Lisa was all smiles as Jana sat down gingerly on the side of her bed.

"Want to play a game?" asked Lisa.

"Maybe," Jana said halfheartedly. She started to

add that she couldn't stay long because she had come to the hospital to visit someone else, then another idea struck her.

"I'll bet it's pretty lonesome in here all by yourself, isn't it?" asked Jana.

Lisa nodded. "Yup."

"And Gorgeous is nice to have around, but he's awfully quiet. Right?"

Lisa looked at her warily and then scooped Gorgeous into her arms and hugged him. "You can't have him. He's *mine*."

Jana started to shout that Gorgeous wasn't Lisa's bear and never had been, then she caught herself. Poor Lisa, she thought, looking closely at the little girl again. Not only did she have a broken leg, but her parents were in another part of the hospital. And Lisa's long blond hair hung limply over her shoulders as if, in spite of the nurses' attempts to brush it, it badly needed a mother's care.

How can I ask for Gorgeous back? wondered Jana. But then her thoughts returned to Randy, lying asleep two floors below. *Everyone needs someone to hug*. Her mother had said that, and so had Mrs. Foss. Well, Randy needs Gorgeous, she thought stubbornly.

"Have any of your relatives gotten here yet?" asked Jana.

Nodding, Lisa loosened her grip on Gorgeous and

looked at Jana. "One . . . two . . . three of them," she said proudly. "They come to see me every day."

"Does it make you feel better to have someone visit you?" asked Jana.

"Sure. Lots better."

"Just the same as Gorgeous made you feel better before your family got here?"

Lisa nodded again, but the wary look had returned to her face.

"Well, I was wondering if you would mind if Gorgeous went to visit someone else in this hospital who is lonesome? He was hurt in an accident, too, and"—she paused as her voice cracked with emotion—"and I think Gorgeous would help him to feel better, just the way he did for you."

Big, solemn eyes stared at Jana, but Lisa did not speak for a moment. "Does he have a cast on his leg?" she asked finally.

"No," said Jana. "But he has bandages wrapped all around his head, and the doctors are having a hard time getting him to wake up."

"Oh," said Lisa.

Jana could tell that Lisa was carefully thinking over what she had just heard.

"I've been talking to him, too," Jana went on. She knew she shouldn't bother to tell Lisa about trying to wake Randy. The little girl was too young to understand. But she couldn't stop the words. "I thought that maybe if he heard my voice, he would open his eyes, but it didn't work."

Lisa put a hand on her side and cocked her head at Jana. "Well, why didn't you say so?" she said. "Gorgeous whispers in my ear and wakes me up all the time. And he tells me secrets, too. He knows lots of secrets, and when he whispers in my ear, it tickles!"

Jana looked at Lisa in astonishment, remembering how annoyed she had been at the little girl for talking to Gorgeous and pretending he was telling her secrets. No, thought Jana, I was more than annoyed. I was jealous. And now, she realized, Lisa was holding out Gorgeous to her and smiling.

"Oh, thank you, Lisa," Jana cried, hugging both Lisa and Gorgeous. "I'll come back and visit you every day. And I'll play games with you, and read stories to you, and do anything you want me to."

"Will you take me for a ride in the wheelchair?" Lisa challenged, her eyes bright with excitement.

"Of course I will . . . if Mrs. Foss says it's okay," she added. "I have to go now, but I'll see you tomorrow. I promise."

"Oh, boy! Oh, *boy*!" Lisa squealed as Jana scooted out the door.

A few minutes later Jana stood inside the quiet room in the intensive care unit. She had explained to Mrs. Kirwan why she hadn't come straight to

Randy's room, and then she had arranged the cards, the banner, and the autographed football on the nightstand where he would be able to see them when he opened his eyes. Now she held Gorgeous in her arms and walked toward the bed.

"I've brought a good friend to stay with you at night and when I'm at school," she began. "It's Gorgeous, and he'll be better than an alarm clock for waking you up. He knows lots of secrets, too, but be careful. When he whispers in your ear, he tickles."

Jana couldn't help smiling as she slid Gorgeous under the covers. At first, she put him on his back beside Randy with his arms reaching into the air. But after she looked at the two of them for a moment, she turned the soft white bear on his side so that his arms held Randy in a gentle hug and his heart-shaped mouth brushed Randy's face with a kiss. Then she tiptoed out of the room.

CHAPTER

15

For the next couple of days, Jana went straight to the hospital after school to visit Lisa, playing games, reading to her, and rolling her up and down the hall in the wheelchair. Then her mother and Pink would pick her up on their way home from work so that she could do her homework and eat supper before one of the Kirwans dropped by to take her with them to see Randy.

Each evening when she tiptoed into his room she hoped to see him sitting up, eyes open and laughing, as he waited for her to come in. But instead, he remained asleep. The only thing that seemed to change was where she would find Gorgeous when she got there. Sometimes he would be in the chair beside Randy's bed. Other times he would be sitting high on Randy's pillow or on the foot of the bed. But always his sweet smile made her spirits lift a little bit. Gorgeous wouldn't let her down. He had always been there when she needed a friend, and each time she left the intensive care unit she snuggled him up beside Randy again.

Sometimes before she went to sleep at night she would think about the accident and all the things that had happened since then, feeling just as confused as ever. First, I was trying to find someone to blame, she thought. But there really isn't anyone to blame for an accident. And I've been trying to find something to do to help. Anything that will make things better, but that hasn't worked, either. Then she would finally fall into a fitful sleep.

On Friday afternoon, when Jana reached the hospital, she was looking forward to seeing Lisa. The little girl had become one of the brightest parts of her day, and Jana knew that she would miss her when she went home. Mrs. Foss had said that it would be soon because Mr. and Mrs. Pratt were getting stronger every day.

Sometimes Lisa's smile made Jana think of Ashley, the baby Taffy Sinclair and she had found on the steps of Mark Twain Elementary last year in sixth

grade. Baby Ashley had been so sweet that she had
captured everybody's heart, and Jana was beginning
to realize that Lisa was just as sweet now that she
was giving the little girl a chance.

To her surprise, Lisa was already sitting in her
wheelchair when Jana got to her room.

"Jana! Jana! You get to take me to visit my
mommy and daddy!" shouted Lisa.

"That's right," said Mrs. Foss, who was smooth-
ing the covers on Lisa's bed. "She went up for a little
while this morning, and I thought maybe you'd like
to take her up to see them this afternoon."

Jana blinked at the nurse. "Me?" she said in a surprised voice. She knew that Lisa had been visiting
them, but she had never expected to be asked to take
the little girl to see them herself.

"Sure. You can handle Lisa as well as any of the
nurses. Besides, you're her special friend. I think
she'd like for you to meet her parents."

"Please," begged Lisa, grabbing Jana's hand and
holding on for dear life.

"Well . . . okay," said Jana. "Fifth floor?"

"That's right," said Mrs. Foss. "Room five oh
seven."

Lisa chattered nonstop all the way up to the fifth
floor. "And my daddy's going to buy me a bicycle as
soon as my leg is well and . . ." she was saying as
Jana knocked on the door to Room 507.

A man's voice called to them to come in, and Jana propped open the door and wheeled Lisa inside, wondering if it wouldn't be best to say a quick hello and duck out so that the family could be alone together.

"Mommy, Daddy, this is Jana!" Lisa shouted the instant she was inside the room.

"Hello, Jana," said the woman in the bed nearest the door. One of her legs was suspended in traction and there was a large bandage on an arm.

"We've been hearing a lot about you," said the man in the second bed. One of his eyes was bandaged and both arms were in casts. "In fact, you and Gorgeous are just about all Lisa can talk about. We can't thank you enough for your kindness and for being so unselfish with your bear. I don't know what Lisa would have done without Gorgeous to love and hold on to while she was alone."

Jana stared at the floor, unable to say anything. How could she tell them that she hadn't wanted Lisa to have Gorgeous and that she had tried every way she could think of to get him back?

Finally she sighed deeply and said, "Actually Lisa is the unselfish one. She's loaned Gorgeous to my friend who is in the intensive care unit on the second floor. He's in a coma."

"And he won't wake up for the doctors, so

Gorgeous is going to tell him secrets and tickle his ear," Lisa announced gleefully.

Jana couldn't help but smile, and she was pleased to see that Mr. and Mrs. Pratt were smiling, too. But suddenly her attention was drawn to a voice coming over the hospital intercom.

"Jana Morgan. If Jana Morgan is in the hospital, will you please come to the intensive care unit on the second floor at once? Jana Morgan to the intensive care unit on the second floor."

"Oh, my gosh," she shouted. "That's me! It must be Randy!" She spun around, looking first at the door and then at Lisa in her panic. "I have to go there! But I can't! I mean, what about Lisa?"

"It's okay," said Mr. Pratt. "We'll call a nurse to take Lisa back to her room. You go ahead."

Jana murmured a quick thank-you and dashed for the elevator. Her heart was pounding as she waited for the doors to open slowly. Riding down to the second floor, she didn't dare wonder why her name had been called. The Kirwans knew that she came to the hospital every afternoon to see Lisa, so if there had been a change in Randy's condition . . . But what kind of change could it be?

The elevator took forever to reach the second floor, stopping at every floor to let people on and off. No one else seemed in a hurry, and Jana wanted to shout at the top of her lungs that she had to get to the intensive care unit fast. That it was *an emergency*.

Finally the elevator stopped at her floor, and Jana got out, breaking into a run as soon as the doors closed behind her.

"I'm here. I'm here," she called as she slid around the corner and caught sight of the nurses' station outside Randy's room.

The red-haired nurse was there again, the one who had sent her away the first time she had tried to see Randy, but this time she looked up and smiled. "Are you Jana Morgan?"

Jana nodded anxiously, feeling as if her heart was going to jump right out of her body.

"You may go right on in," said the nurse.

The door seemed a mile away as Jana headed toward it, but as she pulled it open and looked inside, she couldn't believe her eyes. Randy and Gorgeous were sitting up in bed side by side, both smiling at her and both looking as if they were waiting for a hug.

Jana sat in the fourth-floor lounge holding Gorgeous and waiting for her turn to see Randy again. Now that he was awake and getting better, he had been moved to a room across the hall from the room she had shared with Lisa, and tons of aunts and uncles and cousins had turned up to visit him. She tapped her foot and frowned at the door, wishing they would hurry up. She could hardly wait to talk to him in private.

The doctors had made all sorts of scientific explanations for why Randy had awakened. They had credited medical skill and dedicated doctors with bringing him out of his coma. Jana bounced Gorgeous on her knee and said confidentially, "That's all they know. We know the real reason he woke up. Don't we?"

Gorgeous gave her a conspiratorial smile.

"We did everything we could to make things better," she assured, returning his smile. "You and I *both*."

Her smile faded as she looked at Gorgeous with his shiny black eyes and his sweet, heart-shaped smile. She had the feeling he was trying to tell her something, remind her of something she had forgotten.

"I know. Lisa helped, too," said Jana. "I didn't mean to forget. She let me take you to Randy to make him feel better."

Gorgeous's smile seemed to grow brighter. "And I suppose you've been thinking about how lonely she'll be when she gets home and can't go out to play because of that cast, haven't you?"

Jana thought she saw Gorgeous nod. "And that

maybe you'd like to go home with her and be her friend?"

This time she was certain that he nodded.

"I know Randy wouldn't mind," she added. "He's a kind and sensitive person, just like you, and he'd be proud of you for helping a little girl."

Sighing, Jana gave Gorgeous one last hug and hurried to Lisa's room.

"I still think it was Gorgeous tickling your ear that woke you up," teased Jana. It was later that afternoon and she was finally sitting beside Randy and talking to him in private.

"No," said Randy, shaking his head stubbornly. "What really did it was the dream. I remember it so clearly because you were in it."

"I was in it?" said Jana, screwing up her face in disbelief. "What was I doing?"

"You wouldn't believe it," said Randy, looking suddenly embarrassed. "You would think I'd totally flipped out if I told you."

"Try me," challenged Jana.

Randy looked at her for a moment as if he were trying to get up his nerve. "Okay. Here goes. I was in this forest, see. For some reason I was lying in a huge canopy bed right in the middle of the woods, and there were animals standing around looking at me and birds singing in the trees."

He paused, and Jana felt her eyes turn misty and little prickles dance up her spine. "Go on," she whispered.

"Well, then you came up. You were wearing a long dress and a crown, and you looked just like a princess."

"Then what?" urged Jana. She felt as if she were going to explode.

Randy looked around to make sure no one else was listening before he went on. "Then you kissed me on the cheek and whispered, 'Wake up, Sleeping Handsome.' I know it sounds crazy, but that's really what I dreamed."

Jana wanted to jump up and down and shout for joy, but instead she managed to control her emotions and ask, "Have you told anybody else about this dream?"

"Are you kidding? And you'd better not tell anyone either. Especially Dr. Garza or my parents. Promise?"

Jana smiled slyly. Of course someday she would tell him that it hadn't really been a dream, but not now. She didn't want to take the chance that the doctors would be able to find a scientific explanation for this, too. It was much too wonderful and romantic just the way it was. She doubted that the Kirwans would say anything about her crazy scheme to wake Sleeping Handsome with a kiss, and neither would The Fabulous Five if she asked them not to. So for now, it would be her special secret—until the perfect moment came to tell him the truth.

"Okay. If that's the way you want it," she said. "I promise. *I'll never tell.*"

CHAPTER

16

"I don't know, Katie," Tony said, shaking his head slowly. "Why do you always want to stick your nose into other people's business?"

"Stick my nose into other people's business?" shrieked Katie. Giving her kickstand a vicious boot, she waited an instant until the bike stood on its own and then put her hands on her hips and glared at Tony. "What do you mean by that? She's my own mother, isn't she?"

Tony parked his bike beside Katie's and strolled up the sidewalk to sit down on the Shannon's front steps before answering. "Sure, but suppose she still misses your father and doesn't want to go out on dates? Had you thought about that?"

Katie rolled her eyes heavenward and said patiently, "Of course she still misses my father. But that's not the point. She's a writer, and writers spend most of their time alone, staring at a blank computer screen. I just think that if she had someone to go out and have some fun with, she'd be a lot better off, that's all."

"So, who'd you have in mind?" asked Tony.

"I haven't decided yet," Katie answered matter-of-factly. "But it has to be somebody really nice and a lot of fun. Don't worry. I'll find someone. And I'll probably have to coach her since it's been so long since she's been out on a date."

Tony shook his head again and gazed toward the ground. "There she goes again, folks," he said to no one in particular. "Her Honor, Katie Shannon, champion of the underdog, has picked a new role to play—*Dear Abby*."

Katie made a face. "Don't be disgusting. I know exactly what I'm doing."

But does Katie really know what she's doing? What will happen when Katie tries to help her mother with romance? Find out in *The Fabulous Five #12 Katie's Dating Tips*.

ABOUT THE AUTHOR

Betsy Haynes, the daughter of a former news-woman, began scribbling poetry and short stories as soon as she learned to write. A serious writing career, however, had to wait until after her marriage and the arrival of her two children. But that early practice must have paid off, for within three months Mrs. Haynes had sold her first story. In addition to a number of magazine short stories and the Taffy Sinclair series, Mrs. Haynes is also the author of *The Great Mom Swap* and its sequel, *The Great Boyfriend Trap*. She lives in Colleyville, Texas, with her husband, who is also an author.

Great FREE offer just for you!

Join SNEAK PEEKS™!

Do you want to know what's new before anyone else? Do you like to read great books about girls just like you? If you do, then you won't want to miss SNEAK PEEKS™! Be the first of your friends to know what's hot ... When you join SNEAK PEEKS™, we'll send you FREE inside information in the mail about the latest books ... *before they're published!* Plus updates on your favorite series, authors, and exciting new stories filled with friendship and fun ... adventure and mystery ... girlfriends and boyfriends.

It's easy to be a member of SNEAK PEEKS™. Just fill out the coupon below ... and get ready for fun! It's FREE! Don't delay—sign up today!

IT'S THE FABULOUS FIVE!

From Betsy Haynes, the bestselling author of the Taffy Sinclair books, *The Great Mom Swap,* and *The Great Boyfriend Trap,* comes THE FABULOUS FIVE. Follow the adventures of Jana Morgan and the rest of THE FABULOUS FIVE as they begin the new school year in Wakeman Jr. High.

- [ ] **SEVENTH-GRADE RUMORS (Book #1)** 15625-X $2.75
- [ ] **THE TROUBLE WITH FLIRTING (Book #2)** 15633-0 $2.75
- [ ] **THE POPULARITY TRAP (Book #3)** 15634-9 $2.75
- [ ] **HER HONOR, KATIE SHANNON (Book #4)** 15640-3 $2.75
- [ ] **THE BRAGGING WAR (Book #5)** 15651-9 $2.75
- [ ] **THE PARENT GAME (Book #6)** 15670-5 $2.75
- [ ] **THE KISSING DISASTER (Book #7)** 15710-8 $2.75
- [ ] **THE RUNAWAY CRISIS (Book #8)** 15719-1 $2.75
- [ ] **THE BOYFRIEND DILEMMA (Book #9)** 15720-5 $2.75

Follow the adventures of Jana and the rest of **THE FABULOUS FIVE** in a new series by Betsy Haynes.

Taffy Sinclair is perfectly gorgeous and totally stuck-up. Ask her rival Jana Morgan or anyone else in the sixth grade of Mark Twain Elementary. Once you meet Taffy, life will **never** be the same.

Don't Miss Any of the Terrific Taffy Sinclair Titles from Betsy Haynes!